CAMPUS AMBASSADOR

CAMPUS AMBASSADOR

Looking for a Place to Hide

Written by

LOUIS SHEPPARD

3rd Edition

CAMPUS AMBASSADOR

Notice of Copyright

3rd Edition Published by DreamEmpire Publishing

November 20, 2023

Book Interior Design by - DreamEmpire Publishing

Edited by - Diana Rhodes

Printed in the United States of America

First Printing Edition, Spring 2022

Second Printing Edition, Summer 2022

ISBN Paperback: 9798431876134 |ISBN Hardcover (KDP): 9798852212184

ISBN Hardcover Ingram Spark: 9798990858312

Copywritten with the Library of Congress

To my dear friend, Stanley Bibbs:

A man of many companions may come to ruin,

but there is a friend who sticks closer than a brother.

Proverbs 18:24

ACKNOWLEDGMENTS

I am grateful to Roy Lee Hadnott, Seraphine Aden, Mychika "Missy" Edwards, Michael Otuafo, and Abdul El-Amin Luqman. Their patience and encouragement were invaluable.

I am indebted to Debra "SMILELADY" Johnson for her consistent constructive input. Always with a smile, she encouraged my efforts with timely words of wisdom. I am thankful to Kpoku Simon Amponsah for challenging me to think outside of the box, and LaTaunya Grimes Hays for helping me capture the scenes commonly referred to as *dirty south* with accuracy.

Lastly, a special thanks to Joyce Licorish DreamEmpire publishing for helping me along this journey.

This book is a tribute to their honesty.

FOREWARD

Navigating the complexities of relationships can be a perplexing journey. At times, these connections burn with intensity; at other moments, they're shrouded in ambiguity, or even exist solely in the realm of fantasy.

In "Campus Ambassador," Louis delves into the unspoken bond between Louis, the Ambassador, and Marcie. Louis's gestures - greeting Marcie at the school's main office, guiding her to classes, carrying her books, and occasionally treating her to lunch - transcended mere kindness. These heartfelt acts led Louis to believe he had won the heart of the campus's most admired girl. However, his perception was a mirage, and he was poised to confront a harsh reality.

Through this novel, we explore the perilous terrain of assumptions and the necessity of genuine engagement in life. Louis's journey from an infatuated admirer of Marcie to a young man facing a stark disillusionment illustrates the pitfalls of unverified beliefs. "Campus Ambassador" not only captivates with its unpredictable plot twists but also imparts crucial life lessons on relationships, the wisdom of spending, and the value of respect.

This narrative masterfully interlaces these themes, presenting a richly layered tale that both entertains and educates. It challenges readers to question their assumptions and take charge of their lives, leaving a profound and reflective impact. "Campus Ambassador" is more than a novel; it's an invitation to approach life with open-mindedness and a readiness to face the unknown, and to always remember respect for your elders, and being open to healing and pushing through difficult situations.

Joyce Licorish
DreamEmpire Publishing

INTRODUCTION

She was the most beautiful girl on campus. It was the self-proclaimed ambassador that pursued her with all his might. The campus Ambassador was mesmerized by her radiant brown skin. She was graceful like a butterfly with a beautiful spirit. She was the light of his heart, and the light never dimmed.

Yet, his charm and confidence were not enough to claim the most sought-after girl on campus.

He was hoping to surprise Marcie on his first day back at school, but it was Louis who was surprised. When he discovers the truth about his childhood sweetheart,

it changes his world forever. The Campus Ambassador begins to look for a place to hide.

Forgiving is not about forgetting; it's letting go of the hurt.

- *Mary McCloud Bethune*

TABLE OF CONTENTS

ACKNOWLEDGMENTS 9

FOREWARD 10

INTRODUCTION 12

Chapter 1 5

A Lesson in Courage 5

Chapter 2 11

Puppy Love 11

Chapter 3 16

Pursuit of Happiness 16

Chapter 4 19

The Campus Ambassador 19

Chapter 5 30

Too Much to Bear 30

Chapter 6 38

The Eye of The Tiger 38

Chapter 7 43

The Journey of a Thousand Miles 43

Chapter 8 48

Mountains to Climb 48

Chapter 9 58

Commencement 58

Chapter 10 62

Road Trip 62

Chapter 11......70
Tiger Town 70
Chapter 12......93
Bayou Classic......93
Chapter 13......102
Study Hall 102
Chapter 14......114
The Nicest Guy 114

Chapter 1

A Lesson in Courage

The sky was tinged crimson, with smoke from discharged tear gas canisters littering the streets. Soldiers armed with assault weapons patrolled the streets and alleyways in military vehicles. Strip malls, parking lots, and school zones resembled Saigon. Noise pollution from police helicopters patrolled the skies with blinding floodlights from above.

"Say it Loud" could be heard in the distance as protesters escaped with loaves of bread, cartons of eggs, appliances, electronics, jewelry, crates of liquor, soda pop, and bubblegum.

These were scary times for a minor and his siblings squeezed together in the back seat of their dad's station wagon, navigating through the streets of an urban warfare zone.

As we approached the red light, we noticed an officer manhandling a young woman.

“When the light turns green Ed, be ready to take the wheel.'” My father said with concern to my mother. You see Ed was short for Edna, an affectionate nickname he had given her.

“Moments later, the cracked traffic light turned green. Surprisingly, my father jumped out of the car, ran across the street, and confronted the police officer for accosting the woman, a woman no bigger than a saltshaker in stature. “Excuse me, Officer, why are you accosting this woman?"

“Return to your car, Sir, or you will be placed under arrest for interfering with an officer in the line of duty.”

“I will not,” insisted my dad, “until you explain why you are mistreating this woman who is not resisting.” A National Guardsman standing nearby was surprised when my father approached the arresting officer. Shoulders drawn at attention; my father did not budge.

“Turn around, Sir, you are being placed under arrest for interfering with an officer in the line of duty!”

My dad was ordered to turn around and place his hands on the hood of a parked truck, handcuffed, arrested, and shoved into the backseat of a police squad car. The woman, initially accosted, now was irate. She started yelling and screaming at the Officer. In a split second, she was wrestled to the ground, handcuffed, and arrested along with my dad and taken to jail. Remembering my father's words, my mother quickly went into action, slid over the console to the driver's seat, started the ignition, adjusted her rearview mirror, and proceeded to slowly drive away.

“Damn it,” my mom said, as she slammed her hands on the steering wheel in anger. She was furious. We all witnessed the arrest. A growing crowd of onlookers were also furious, demanding justice in unison. *How did my father know he would be handcuffed, arrested, and carted off to jail?* I wondered.

As my mother adjusted the rearview mirror, she checked the backseat, making sure we all had our seat belts properly fastened, making eye contact with all her four children, trying to maintain calm in a volatile situation.

Things happened so quickly that day, but one thing for sure that will be indelibly etched in my mind, is how my father stood in defense of a perfect stranger. On that day, I was proud of my father and proud to be his son.

My mother, in her own right, was a warrior and calmly drove us home that afternoon. "We will be home shortly," she assured us.

Minutes later, she pulled into the driveway, turned off the engine, paused for a moment, took a long deep breath, pressed her forehead against the steering wheel, and started sobbing and praying all at once. We all followed suit in the back seat. A memorable moment for a five-year-old boy and his siblings who, except for one, were not much older.

Once inside, "Time to go to bed, children," she directed.

"But we haven't eaten all day," we complained in unison.

Amidst the chaotic day, my mother had totally forgotten we had not eaten. After we were picked up from school, we found ourselves in a traffic jam of fire trucks, emergency vehicles, and people dashing through the streets. "You promised us that no matter what, you would never send us to bed without dinner."

"Yah mom, I am hungry, too," I sniffled.

"You're right," she responded. "Okay, this evening, because of time, you will not have your usual full-course meal. Instead, you can have peanut butter and jelly sandwiches, or grilled cheese sandwiches, chocolate milk or Kool-Aid, and a piece of fruit," she ordered. "Then you will go to bed, but not before you brush your teeth and say your prayers. And remember to pray for your father who will be coming home soon." After we ate, bathed, said our prayers, we all went to bed.

My father, meanwhile, spent the night in jail. Protesters, social activists, the unemployed, homeless, and lawbreakers all crammed into a single holding tank. Blood, sweat, and tears dampened the jail cell floor and faces of the detainees. Some knelt in prayer, others meditated, a few chatted in protest, while others sobbed from nightfall to daybreak.

Bedtime was restless for mom; she didn't sleep a wink. She spent the entire night up and down pacing the floor. I could faintly hear her sobbing through the paper-thin walls. My father being incarcerated was a first in our family. My father, a retired military man, was a law-abiding citizen. Still, my mother was worried. She spent the waking hours recollecting stories from church members, friends, and neighbors arrested and later released. She knew the jailhouse horror stories vividly and was nervous.

The following morning, she made us turkey bacon, eggs, and toast. She hardly spoke, except for leading us in morning prayer. Clearly, she was agitated and edgy, but overall remained optimistic that things would be alright.

The following afternoon, my father was released from the county jail. She, along with my elder brother, were among the first at the county jail the following morning to greet him. My mother waited eagerly in the lobby with other families. Her heart skipped a beat when he appeared, unharmed and seemingly in good spirits. First, he had to sign a 'Notice to Appear" before being released from custody. Without uttering a single word, they embraced. With tears in her eyes she said, "Are you okay, my husband?"

"I am fine," he responded.

Once safely in the car, seatbelts fastened, she wailed. "Why do you always have to get involved in other folks' business? You didn't even know that woman, but you stuck your neck out, literally, in her defense. But she didn't even say 'Thank you'."

My mother was livid. My father sat quietly and listened, contemplating her every word. When she finished, he leaned over and gave her a gentle kiss on the cheek.

"Sorry," he whispered. "That woman was not 'other folks', she was 'my folks, 'our folks. I pray to God, someone will do the same, if you were in the same situation." he responded. "Doing the right thing can be risky; a risk we must take sometimes."

In the prophetic words of Dr. Martin Luther King Jr., my father responded, "Injustice anywhere is a threat to justice everywhere."

"I am just glad you are back home and safe, my husband." She exhaled and smiled. They embraced again.

Later that evening, while spending some time alone, my parents shared a decision-making moment together. "The inner city is getting increasingly dangerous, National Guardsmen, state troopers, military vehicles patrolling the streets, sporadic gunfire, and buildings ablaze," this is no place to raise a family," declared my mother. "Time for us to move."

Holding her breath, she peered into my father's eyes searching for a response. To her surprise, she didn't have to wait long. "Yes, I agree," he responded emphatically. "There is a time for everything. Now is the right time for us to move."

She released a sigh of relief. "Hallelujah," she shouted.

Weeks later, we were packed and ready to leave the city; 35 miles eastbound towards no-man's land. Destination, an unincorporated town that later became San Dimas.

My parents were happy with the decision to leave the city. Our new residence was fabulous. Lemon and orange groves, and strawberry vines bearing ginormous fruit freely lined the roadside. A 'citrus heaven' my mother would say after indulging in a fresh bowl of fresh fruit salad.

Horses and cows peacefully grazed the hillside. Squirrels, possums, and burrowing rodents with furry-lined pouches playfully darted in and around tractors and bulldozers constructing new homes and roads.

Thanks to my father's military service record, we were able to qualify for the G.I bill; a bill that helped qualifying veterans and their families. Housing was one fabulous benefit for those who served in the armed services with an honorable discharge. Little did they know that social challenges, divisiveness, evident in the inner city, had buried itself deep like rodents, had scared the unincorporated town and had spread throughout the inland Empire and beyond. But amidst brewing unsettledness, in our new town, I found something special.

Chapter 2

Puppy Love

I found puppy love in the second grade at Robert Ekstrand Elementary School. An unfamiliar sensation consumed me every time I was in the presence of Mrs. Gonzales, my second-grade teacher. Her fun-loving spirit, mesmerizing skin tone, curvaceous lips, and her warm smile hypnotized an entire second-grade class. But for me, Mrs. Gonzales was just a good, fun-loving, beautiful, brown-skin Latina with a gift for teaching.

Watching her standing at the chalkboard, teaching, was spellbinding for a seven-year-old. Learning became a fun experience in Mrs. Gonzales' class. I looked forward to going to school hearing her voice, "Okay, students, time to line up, recess is over."

Her voice was mesmerizing to my ears. I would make a point to be first in line even if I had to bully my way through. It was a happy feeling in Mrs. Gonzales' class. I always paid attention, hanging on her every word and found myself constantly craving her attention. So occasionally, I would be disruptive in class just to get it. I simply loved the attention. It made my young heart flutter. The only thing that I disliked in her class was when other students followed my lead and became unruly. Mrs. Gonzales recognized my leadership abilities and appointed me class Sergeant-at-Arms. I loved it! It gave me a leadership role in the class and on the playground. Every day, five minutes before class ended, I would stand in front of the class, routinely clap my hands twice and shout, "Okay class, it is cleanup time. Pick up all trash on and near your desk, put your chairs on top of your desk, and stand quietly and wait for dismissal." This was my daily script given to me by Mrs. Gonzales and I never deviated. Occasionally, I would notice, out of the corner of my eye, Mrs. Gonzales' smile of approval. She was cultivating leadership in one of her students.

All this slowed down when I got the bright idea, voluntarily, to give Mrs. Gonzales a hand-made display table for Christmas. On the way to school, I would detour, hop the fence of a neighbor's fence without their permission, without permission, and pick plums and oranges to take to school. All for Mrs. Gonzales.

"Thank you," she would always say with a smile. She was appreciative, and I was happy. Always seeking attention, seeking approval from my second-grade teacher.

One day, shortly after lunch, a gentleman in a police uniform entered the class with a birthday cake in hand. Mrs. Gonzales' face lit up. You could tell she was pleasantly surprised.

The police officer moved the fruit from the hand-made table, placed the fruit I had just picked, on a nearby counter reserved for construction paper, paint, and paintbrushes, placed the cake on the hand-made wooden table, and lit twenty-seven birthday candles. The class stood up, the policeman joined hands with Mrs. Gonzales, and we all sang Happy Birthday to my favorite teacher. Mrs. Gonzales proudly introduced the Officer, "Class, this is Mr. Gonzales, my husband." My heart instantly sank.

Blankness shrouded my mind. At the tender age of seven, even puppy-love can be unsettling.

At the end of the day, unceremoniously, I took my hand-made table, a brown paper bag filled with carefully selected uneaten fruit, and slowly walked home. I told Mrs. Gonzales I was no longer interested in serving as class Sergeant-at-Arms.

After that, I became a real class clown.

Verbal reprimand, recess detention, clean-up, even being sent to the Counselor's office, was not an effective deterrent to my unruly behavior.

Things suddenly changed when Mrs. Gonzales initiated a home parent-teacher meeting. "Spoke to Mrs. Gonzales today," my mother reported, ''She says you have to serve after-school detention tomorrow for disruptive class behavior. Is that true? I thought Mrs. Gonzales was your favorite teacher, why suddenly are you misbehaving in her class? She even suggested a home visit to talk to both me and your father."

I panicked. I did not want Ms. Gonzales coming to my house; I especially did not want her talking to my father about my class behavior. My father had little patience for misbehavior in school. I didn't want him to be angry. His punishment was always excessive; washing windows, pulling weeds, trimming thorny rose bushes were among the typical household chores. A hard head, my parents would often say," makes a soft, tender behind." And if that didn't work, my behind was always a soft spot for adjustment.

The thought of Mrs. Gonzales making a home visit was painfully unthinkable. I had to make a change quickly!

Both my father and mother had no patience for misbehavior. The day before the scheduled home visit, I was sent on an errand to the grocery store to fetch bread, eggs, cereal, and the *Daily Progress Bulletin,* my mother's favorite newspaper. On the way to the store, I ran into a classmate named Shirley. “Hello, Louis,” said Shirley. "Everyone in class misses your fruit, especially me. I loved the plums; they were pretty and delicious. Can you bring more please?' she pleaded.

In this revised version, the narrative is adjusted to be in the first person, as if Louis, the main character of your teen drama novella, is telling the story:

"I was happy to learn that my classmates enjoyed the fruit as well, although it was intended for Mrs. Gonzales. At that moment, I decided to resume bringing fruit to school, not for Mrs. Gonzales, but because of Shirley, my classmate, my new puppy-love.

Shirley was nice, with a precious smile. She wore pigtails, with pink and yellow ribbons in her hair. She was the class secretary and well-respected. In class, as part of her secretarial duties, Shirley often escorted me to the counselor's office. She knew I tended to get into trouble in class. But she never commented about my behavior. She seemed to just enjoy our one-on-one conversation while walking to the office. And I was happy she enjoyed the fruit. Unbeknownst to Shirley, I decided to make her my girlfriend.

Shirley came from a very religious household. I insisted on walking her home after school even though her mother suspiciously glared out the front window. We sat and talked till dark sometimes, laughing, joking, eating plums, and watching the sunset. Shirley’s mother suspiciously watched from the window, keeping a close watch on the “Puppy love” on the front porch, with a bag of purple plums. I had a friend, non-judgmental, easy to talk to, pretty, and my own age, my classmate.

With a new puppy love, my behavior miraculously changed. Suddenly I was a model student; polite and courteous. Mrs. Gonzales noticed the new attraction between her student leaders, Shirley and me, and the improved behavior and was happy.

One day, I finally had the courage to sit next to Shirley on the school bus on a field trip. Shirley was uncomfortable; she quickly grabbed her backpack and switched seats. I felt dejected. The bus trip back to school was jovial; classmates laughing, having fun, sharing field trip experiences. For whatever reasons, Shirley was oblivious to me the entire trip. I was noticeably sulky and uneasy. It was an uncomfortable bus experience. It proved to be the longest bus trip ever, with no place to hide.

The experience destroyed the affection I had for Shirley. But more importantly, I lost a special classmate, a good friend. Elementary school puppy-love was a forgettable experience; an experience I chose to avoid in junior high school. Instead, I turned my attention to sports and athletics."

Chapter 3

Pursuit of Happiness

After puppy love, sports became my interest while still in elementary school. Anything involving bodily contact or competitive activity became my pursuit of happiness. I successfully participated in "Punt Pass and Kick," a skillful competition offered by the National Football League, POP Warner Football, a youth football organization that requires its participants to maintain standards in order to participate, and Little League baseball and softball, the world's largest organized youth sports program throughout the United States.

Before school hours every morning, the boys at Robert Ekstrand Elementary School would often play 'Kill the Man with the ball'; a game much the same as flag football. An unsupervised, innovative game played by elementary school kids. A game where I would run as fast as I could, as long as I could with the football, avoiding other boys until exhausted and then relinquish the ball to someone else. One rule - No tackling. Kids could catch me. I laughed and joked the whole time while being chased with the ball in hand, avoiding the kids gracefully with ease.

Unexpectedly, I was blind-sided and tackled from behind by a boy, nearly twice my size. I screamed in pain; my leg contorted backward as I fell to the ground, with the weight of the assailant smashing me to the ground. I fell awkwardly with the weight of my assailant and several other boys piling on top of me. "Get off of me!" I screamed. I grimaced in pain. From the expression on the faces of the boys, it was serious. The game stopped. The morning playground supervisor noticed me on the ground grimacing in pain, crying with my leg twisted backward with kids gathered around. He immediately radioed the nurse's office, who rushed to the scene.

The nurse was shocked. "The bone is protruding from his pant leg," observed the nurse. "This is serious." Administration was alerted, and the Fire Department was contacted. The scene was sickening. Some students regurgitated their lunch at the site of it. Students were dispersed and directed to return to class. Minutes later, an ambulance and medical vehicles arrived on the scene, and I was whisked away in an ambulance to the hospital.

Once at the hospital, I was rushed to X-rays. The radiologist determined I had a mid-femur fracture. The doctor scanned the X-rays and determined I required emergency surgery, scheduled for the following morning. My mother and father were at my bedside for surgery and throughout. A pin was inserted in my left femur, and doctors determined the surgery was a success. I was in the recovery ward two hours after surgery and was later moved to the orthopedic ward for two days. The physical therapist instructed me on how to use crutches and the "do's and don'ts" to help expedite my recovery. I was discharged from the hospital after two weeks.

At home, I was able to move about gingerly with the aid of crutches. My competitive interest never wavered. At home, I watched plenty of television, track and field, and football. Watching sports on television fueled my continued interest in sports. I was finally released from doctor's care and allowed to return to school with limited physical fitness activities. It wasn't long before I was running, jumping, and playing with the other kids in the neighborhood and school.

The next few years were a blur as I grew and thrived through middle school, maintaining a keen interest in athletics. My competitive nature was ever increasing, propelling me into the world of sports as I made my transition into high school where I became the 'Campus Ambassador'.

Chapter 4

The Campus Ambassador

The front office on any high school campus is normally quiet and professional. However, on Fridays at Garey High School, the front office was quite the opposite. Garey High was the jewel of the Pomona Unified School District. Office aides came highly recommended by staff. Many were honor roll candidates with exemplary citizenship. The front office at Garey High was the happiest place on campus for students, particularly on a Friday morning. On Fridays, the vibe in the main office was upbeat and filled with lively student chatter of campus gossip and rumors. The office aides proudly referred to the main office as Freestyle Friday. Student aides created a jovial office atmosphere. With the radio blaring, students hummed to the best of Marvin Gaye, The Whispers, and The Temptations. The front office became known as the happiest place on campus.

The bell rang to start the first period. Students streamed into the main office requesting re-admit slips or needing to use the phone. Louis was an office aide who wore his blue and gold

Varsity letterman jacket with pride. He came midyear last year to Garey High and now was the only sophomore on the varsity football team. Garey High's football team was loaded with great athletes. It was rare for a sophomore to make the cut. However, Louis' short, stocky athletic body gave him the talent he needed to earn a spot on the team. So, he proudly wore his letterman jacket in the office for all to see.

Louis' primary duty post in the main office was the front counter. Greeting substitute teachers and new incoming students were his most important office responsibilities. Louis performed his official duties with care and precision just as he would with any play on the football field. It was his responsibility to ensure substitute teachers received their room assignments, sub-folders, a map of the campus and classroom keys. Louis was conscientious about his office duties. He was always stuffing and organizing folders for the substitute teachers. When he greeted substitute teachers, he proudly referred to himself as The Campus Ambassador. Louis and the other office aides made sure the main office ran like clockwork, even on Fridays without administrative supervision.

One Friday morning, an unfamiliar face graced the entrance to the main office. It was not a parent nor a substitute teacher. It was a new student. All the student aides, including Louis, froze and turned their attention to the student. Even the girls were astonished and took notice of the stranger.

A short, shapely, and beautifully brown girl entered the office wearing a miniskirt. Louis sat staring stolidly at the office entrance. Instantly, Louis forgot about his office duties.

The office ceiling fans were not enough to cool the beads of perspiration upon his brow. Normally cool, calm, and collected, Louis was now uneasy. This new girl confidently stepped to the front counter directly in front of Louis. With only the front counter separating them, everything seemed to stop. Time stood still. Freestyle Friday's atmosphere suddenly ceased. The radio was turned down to a civil tone.

Louis asked her, "Can I help you?"

She responded, "Yes, my name is Marcie Howard. I am a new student. I need to speak to a counselor to get my class schedule."

Another office aide chimed in and asked, "Counselors are normally assigned by grade level. What grade are you in?"

"I am a freshman," Marcie replied.

Louis inquired, "Where are you from?"

"I am from Los Angeles. My sister, brother, and I are coming from Jefferson High School. We are all enrolling today. They will be coming in shortly," replied Marcie.

"Welcome to Garey High School, Home of The Vikings," Louis said proudly in his ambassador's voice.

"I need to see a counselor. I need to get my class schedule," said Marcie.

"The counselors are in a meeting but should be out shortly. Please have a seat." Louis offered.

All eyes were glued on Marcie. She strolled from the office counter to the chairs. Louis was mesmerized. He was no longer focused on his official duties and responsibilities. Louis was only focused on Marcie. As she walked to her seat, Louis noticed her shapely athletic legs. Marcie had the hips of a mature young woman. She had a small waist and cute feet with red toenail polish. Marcie was easy on the eyes. Louis was instantly hypnotized by her grace and beauty. When the administrative team meeting finally adjourned, Louis quickly ushered Marcie to the Freshman Counselor's office.

Time moved quickly. Louis was hoping Marcie's meeting with the counselor would be over before the bell rang for dismissal. Moments later, Marcie emerged from the counselor's office with her class schedule in hand.

"Got it!" Marcie said triumphantly as she waved her schedule in the direction of Louis. "But I don't know the campus layout," Marcie said in a frustrated tone. She needed someone to show her around the campus, maybe even escort her to class. Louis the Ambassador was the perfect person.

"No worries, I will show you around," Louis said proudly adjusting his blue and gold varsity letterman jacket. Louis demonstrated his good home training and graciously opened the office door for Marcie. He knew how to be a gentleman even away from home and church where he served as an usher.

"Why thank you, Sir. You are such a gentleman," said Marcie. She was polite and well-mannered, too. Marcie smiled and Louis' heart skipped a beat. It was the first time Louis saw Marcie's soft dimples and gorgeous smile. By this time, it was obvious Louis had a twinkle in his eye for the new girl. Clearly, the attraction was strong.

Marcie inquired, "And your name is?"

"My name is Louis, but I refer to myself as The Campus Ambassador, but you can call me whatever you like,' Louis responded with a sheepish smile. Marcie continued, "Pleasure to meet you Louis or Mr. Ambassador. What shall I call you?"

"Just call me Louis," he said.

Louis proudly walked Marcie to her first-period class. "Here you are. This is your first-period class. Mr. Rasshan is your history teacher. I will be back at the end of the period and walk you to your second class. I don't want you to get lost. This is a big school and it's not always friendly to newcomers, especially girls as beautiful as you. I will serve as your tour guide for today," Louis said with a smile. Louis was flirting and Marcie seemed to enjoy his confidence.

The students were working when Marcie entered through the doorway. The class turned and stared. The girls had a snobbish look on their faces while the boys were gawking. Mr. Rasshan introduced Marcie and assigned her a seat. When the period ended, Louis was waiting for Marcie outside the class.

Walking the halls of Garey High as a new student on the campus was an experience even with a familiar face as an escort. All the students, male and female, took notice of the stranger. Marcie strolled proudly through the halls alongside Louis. The boys were fixated on her pretty face and shapely hips. The girls were standoffish and snobbish.

For nearly two weeks, every period of every day, Louis volunteered to serve as Marcie's escort. The two looked good together. She even volunteered her phone number. Louis felt special. To him, she was his girlfriend. His eyes and attention were always on Marcie, whether in class or on the football field.

Normally, Louis hung out with his fellow teammates during lunch hour and snack break. However, when Marcie arrived at Garey High, Louis spent all his free time with her. During lunch, the two would sit together, laughing and talking. Occasionally, with his mouth gaping open, Louis waited with anticipation while Marcie fed him hot chili cheese fries - one fry at a time. The two were a perfect couple. They were the talk of the town in the campus gossip column.

When Louis was not daydreaming about Marcie, he could be found at school in the gymnasium lifting weights. At home, he pulled weeds in the yard with his older brother or sold newspapers door-to-door making pocket change. He spent his savings lavishly on Marcie's desires.

***

On Labor Day, Louis wanted to surprise Marcie with something special, a gift. He decided to get her a compact electric roller set that is designed to achieve curls and waves. When Louis first saw the roller set in a fashion magazine, he knew instantly Marcie would love it. There was just one problem. The compact electric roller set was beyond Louis' means. Although Louis had saved his earnings, he still did not have enough money to buy the gift.

Early on Saturday morning, two neighborhood friends Tony and Mark decided to go to a local discount store to do window shopping. Louis went along for the ride. Tony had a driver's license and owned a used yellow Volkswagen. The boys squeezed into the Volkswagen looking for a shopping adventure.

Mark was wearing his normal attire - a long shiny black trench coat with platform shoes. His slim frame and greasy Jheri curl was often laughable. His appearance attracted attention wherever he went. Tony had his own unique style. He liked the hippie look of a colorful short sleeve Hawaiian shirt, gray cargo shorts, and open-toe sandals. Louis wore a silver oversized button-up windbreaker jacket, a black dress shirt, and a black Raiders hat. He was always well-groomed with a Quo Vadis haircut and the latest tennis shoes.

When the three entered the store, Louis scanned the store for employees and security staff.

The store was virtually empty, no customers in sight. Only one cashier and a security guard were both busy stocking shelves. The store manager was in his office on the phone. A plan came to Louis' mind in a flash. Being a boy of quick decisions, Louis unbuttoned his windbreaker. He stuffed the roller set under his armpit inside his windbreaker undetected. Then he proceeded to browse the store.

After browsing several aisles with no employees or customers in sight, Louis felt at ease. He exhaled a sigh of relief. Then suddenly, he felt anxious. Out of nowhere, a young woman dressed in a blue staff shirt appeared in the aisle pretending to shop. Her eyes darted back and forth in his direction, occasionally giving a suspicion. Louis was on edge. He felt as though he was being watched, even possibly under surveillance by store security or cameras. Perhaps even the woman in the blue staff shirt was watching him. Louis' breathing became labored. He no longer felt at ease. The pit of his stomach was churning with fear. He started to perspire.

Louis was a known risk taker, always ready to embrace his instincts. Even with a store employee only a few feet away in the same aisle, Louis gambled. He walked straight to the store exit with the merchandise under his jacket. Instinctively, Tony and Mark followed Louis. Just as the boys exited the store, a voice of authority loud enough to echo came from the open doorway, "Excuse me young man. Please, come back inside the store."

Louis was terrified. He knew it was him the store Manager was talking to. The worst imaginable thoughts ran through his mind. If Louis returned to the store and was subsequently searched by security or the manager, he knew he would be busted for shoplifting.

A familiar voice shouted, "Run!"

The boys immediately took off running at top speed, darting through the parking lot until they reached Tony's yellow Volkswagen. Out of breath, the boys jumped in the car. The stolen merchandise was still in Louis' possession stuffed inside his silver oversized windbreaker.

Tony zigzagged his Volkswagen through the sparsely filled parking lot until he reached the street. Driving as fast as possible, Tony sped back toward the neighborhood. The boys heard police sirens in the distance. Afraid he might get caught and that his parents would find out, Louis shouted, "Faster! Faster!"

When they reached the neighborhood, Tony parked the car in the driveway. They sighed with relief, exited the vehicle, and walked toward Tony's house. Tony unlocked and opened the front door.

Suddenly, a police car pulled up in the driveway right behind the Volkswagen. There were no sirens, just bright swirling red lights. The front door of the house was slightly ajar when the officers stepped out of the squad car with their weapons drawn.

With pistols still drawn, the officers invited themselves into the house, following closely behind the boys. The boys were visibly shaken, especially Louis who had the stolen property in his possession. The officers stood like giants with handcuffs dangly, and police batons on their hips were more than enough to frighten teenage boys.

"Have a seat boy," one officer insisted, "Who lives here?"

"I live here. This is my mother's house," responded Tony.

The officer continued, "And whose yellow Volkswagen is that in the driveway you boys just got out of?"

"That is my car," answered Tony. The Interrogation had started.

The officer continued, "Relax, boys. We just got a call that three boys were possibly shoplifting in the local discount store. You boys know anything about that?"

The boys said nothing.

The second officer used the house phone to call back to the store. He spoke to the manager for a description of the suspect. Louis realized his embroidered Raiders hat could make him the prime suspect. He slowly removed the cap from his head and stuffed it underneath the couch. The officer noticed Louis' actions and said, "Stand up, young man!"

The officer retrieved the Raiders hat from under the couch. Louis was promptly searched and found in possession of store merchandise. The officer continued, "You are under arrest! Turn around!"

Louis was handcuffed and escorted out of the house by the officers. They stuffed him into the back seat of the police car. Louis knew his parents would eventually find out. Louis knew once his father found out things would be especially bad.

Louis was tossed in a holding cell at the police station. He was shivering in fear. His mother was immediately contacted. She arrived at the station within minutes. She wondered why on earth is my son in a holding cell at the local police station.

Mrs. Sheppard was a reasonable woman who was prepared to listen to both sides. As a mother, she always gave her children the benefit of the doubt. Innocent until proven otherwise was her motto. However, the evidence was indisputable. The arresting officer calmly gave Mrs. Sheppard a full report of the incident. Louis was finally escorted by the jailer to see his mother. Louis bowed his head in shame when he saw the disgust in his mother's eyes.

"I apologize for my son's behavior," pleaded Mrs. Sheppard, as she squeezed her son's hand angrily.

Since there were no eyewitnesses and no surveillance camera footage, Louis decided to create his own truth. "It wasn't me Mommy," Louis pleaded, "it was Mark." Louis thought blaming Mark was a good idea. Mark had a track record throughout the neighborhood. Mark was known as the neighborhood kleptomaniac.

Confident in her son's explanation, Mrs. Sheppard responded to the allegations, "My son is not a thief. He does not have a record of stealing. Officer, I assure you this is the first and last time my son will be locked up for anything."

Louis was released into his mother's custody. Louis knew his release was not going to be the end of his consequences. He still had to live with this shame in the Sheppard household. So, he decided to cover his tracks.

The next day, even though Louis was on punishment and confined to the house, he still sneaked around the corner to get his story straight with Mark. Louis tapped on Mark's bedroom window and whispered, "If my father comes around here asking who was stealing at the discount store, you be sure to say it was you."

Mark agreed. Mark knew his mother would be lenient with him. After all, Mark was from a single-parent household. He had one sibling. Mark was the mischievous one. His mother was a registered nurse who often worked 24-hour shifts. She was exhausted when she got home. She was a sweet woman who was just unable to effectively monitor and supervise her son's behavior.

Louis, on the other hand, came from a two-parent household with strict house rules and high expectations. There was almost always an adult present at the Sheppard residence. When Louis' parents were occasionally absent at the same time, his older brother Michael was in charge.

The Sheppard household was headed by Mr. Sheppard, a former military police officer with the United States Army. What was highly regarded above all else and expected in the Sheppard family was honesty and education. “Get your education,” Mr. Sheppard preached, “it is the one thing they cannot take away from you.” and always tell the truth”

Education was the key to success, but a career in stealing and lying was the quickest path to jail and punishment. Stealing was unacceptable, shameful and an embarrassment to the entire family. The only person who knew the truth, outside of the arresting officer, store manager, Tony, and Mark, was Clarice, Louis’ younger sister.

Although Clarice was not present when Louis was arrested, she heard what happened from neighbors who witnessed Louis in handcuffs being carted off to jail. The grapevine was the fastest and most accurate source of news in the neighborhood. Clarice confirmed the accounts directly from the horse’s mouth – Louis, himself. Clarice was loyal, soft-spoken, quiet and knew how to keep secrets. She was sworn to secrecy, and so it was.

Chapter 5

Too Much to Bear

In the Sheppard household stealing, slothfulness, and poor academic performance were unacceptable. Louis turned to his big brother for guidance. The greatest influence in Louis' life growing up was his big brother Michael. Louis admired and revered his big brother. Michael was affectionately called Big Mike because of his size. He was a giant compared to Louis. At 17 years old, Big Mike was 6'3" and 220 pounds of solid muscle. Big Mike was adamant about fitness, and it rubbed off on his younger brother. Michael was in many ways Louis' first mentor and role model.

Lifting weights was Big Mike's passion. It was where he found inner peace and tranquility. Big Mike could often be found outside in the backyard lifting weights shirtless. Sometimes, even in the rain, Big Mike urged Louis to join him. Thanks to Big Mike, lifting weights became Louis' pastime. Big Mike was also Louis' first coach and personal trainer. Big Mike taught Louis how to breathe properly while working out. Louis learned how to use the correct form when lifting weights.

At the age of twelve, Louis developed a competitive interest in weightlifting and began to excel in athletics. Football was the sport for which Louis received his most recognition and accolades. Thanks to Big Mike, Louis decided to no longer run from the law. Instead, he decided to play football. Because of his brother, Louis took an interest in souped-up fast cars.

Big Mike loved fast cars. Less than two miles away from where they lived, The Winternationals sports event was held yearly and broadcast live on ABC's Wide-World of Sports. This quarter-mile raceway was the location where some of the fastest dragsters in the country competed. Literally, you could hear the roar of the crowds and the noise from the roaring engines just miles away. Although Big Mike never attended The Winternationals, he watched the competition on television faithfully with enthusiasm alongside of his little brother.

Big Mike was a proud owner of a Dodge Charger and a Dodge Super Bee. He fixed up the Dodge Super Bee to look like and run like a dragster. Louis loved to be in the passenger seat. He loved feeling the power of the engine when Big Mike accelerated on the highway. Watching Big Mike shift gears was fascinating to Louis. Louis wanted to learn how to drive and pleaded with Big Mike for lessons. Thanks to Big Mike, Louis knew how to drive a car by the age of fourteen.

There were times when Louis was not interested in fast cars or lifting weights. At other times, Louis just wanted to play and be mischievous. He was a practical jokester at every opportunity and a nuisance to Big Mike. One weekend, Louis and Big Mike were assigned to wash the outdoor windows. Louis was required to hold the ladder steady while Big Mike climbed up and down the ladder with soap and water from the bucket below. Louis thought it would be funny to position the bucket where Big Mike would step into the cold soapy water. Louis' plan worked to perfection. Big Mike nearly fell. Soapy water splashed everywhere. Louis thought that was the funniest thing and he roared with laughter. Big Mike did not think the stunt was so funny. Big Mike quickly commenced punching his little brother repeatedly while fussing at him the whole time. Louis was laughing so hard he barely felt Big Mike's blows. Aside from learning how to take a punch, Louis eventually learned to love weightlifting and fast cars just like Big Mike.

Still, nothing was more important to Louis than lifting weights and football. With Big Mike's help and training, Louis easily made Garey's football team. Louis was always the first player dressed for practice, out of the locker room and onto the field. Even as a sophomore on a team of speedsters and superstars, Louis was always first in the warmup drills. In the weight room he took pride in being one of the strongest on a team of upperclassmen.

Slowly things began to change after Marcie arrived at Garey. Louis developed a habit of being late to class. He got caught in tardy-sweeps and was assigned after-school detention. This trouble was due to Louis designating himself as Marcie's daily escort to class. Coaches noticed Louis' name frequently on the after-school detention list. Louis was chastised by the coaches for being late to or being absent from football practice. His teammates teased him as he ran extra wind-sprints as punishment for his behavior. He was losing favor with the coaching staff.

He missed school three days in a row due to the flu. He was bedridden under his doctor's care. Plenty of fluids and warm chicken soup was prescribed by his doctor. He lost strength and endurance in three short days. However, Louis never lost his strength and endurance for his Marcie. He could not wait to return to school. He dearly missed her smile, her voice, and her touch. Louis knew she missed him as well. He wrote dozens of love letters which were found by his mother wadded up in the trashcan next to his bed. Over those three bedridden days, writing letters to Marcie improved Louis' writing skills.

Louis and Marcie talked on the phone daily, but the conversations were always brief. She was always busy. She did share with him that she had decided to try out for the freshman cheerleader squad. Louis thought this was a great idea. Surely the freshman squad could use a new pair of pretty legs and another dazzling smile. Usually, the freshman cheerleaders joined the varsity cheerleaders during home games. So, this would be another opportunity for Louis to see Marcie in a short cheerleader's outfit.

Drinking fluids and eating chicken soup with saltine crackers rapidly improved Louis' health. The flu-like symptoms slowly disappeared over those three days. Louis was finally well enough to return to school. He needed to see his Marcie. When he arrived on campus, he immediately went to the office for his re-admit slip and then dashed off to her first period. The class had just been dismissed. The halls were bustling with students. Louis was just in time, he thought, to escort Marcie to the second period. He was hoping to surprise Marcie on his first day back to school, but it was Louis who was surprised. Through the crowded hallways, Louis could easily see Marcie walking with another guy. Louis recognized the new guy as a member of the freshman football team. A freshman, Louis thought to himself, nothing to be alarmed about. Still, Louis was jealous.

Marcie and this new guy were walking together and talking. They were so engaged that Marcie failed to notice Louis was standing less than ten feet away from her in the hallway. Louis was heartbroken. He decided to follow them to second period. The two were still walking together. When Marcie finally reached her class and entered the doorway, she turned and gleefully waved goodbye to the new guy.

"See you next period," the new guy shouted and dashed off to his class. Louis was in shock. His eyes blazed in anger. He had only been away for three days. Now Marcie was with someone else, a freshman at that! Louis' ego was deflated. He decided to show up the following period, but he was too late. The new guy was already there waiting to greet Marcie as soon as she exited the class. Louis was more embarrassed when several of his teammates observed his girl with another guy. Louis felt the weight of the world upon him. In his investigation, Louis learned the new guy was an underclassman, named Marcus Thomas. Marcus was muscular like Louis but taller and thinner.

Weeks passed. Marcie and Marcus were always together like two love birds. During lunch, Louis now sat alone and out of sight in front of the school near a cluster of untrimmed hedges. He felt humiliated, dejected, and embarrassed. He wanted to remain out of sight as much as possible. One day after third period, Louis noticed Marcus and Marcie during the fifteen-minute snack break. They were at Garey's snack shack together hugging. The two would go on to be voted 'Best Couple' in the yearbook.

Freestyle Fridays in the front office continued to be the best place on campus. However, this was no longer the case for Louis. The main office was filled with jokes and laughter about how a freshman had snatched the campus ambassador's girl. Suddenly, school was not so friendly for Louis. He felt more like a loser than an ambassador. Louis moped from class to class alone.

One day, Louis came home disillusioned with school. He was dejected and tired of studying. "I don't like school," he protested. He decided to focus his attention back on football and lifting weights. For the first time in weeks, Louis was punctual to football practice.

Unfortunately, the damage had already been done. Louis had missed so many practices that his playing time on the depth-chart had diminished. He had lost favor with the coaches. They questioned his commitment to the game of football and the team. Once considered next year's team captain and superstar, Louis now found himself a full-time bench warmer. Louis was crushed.

Meanwhile, Marcie made the freshman cheer squad. Her time after school was spent practicing. On game days, she enthusiastically would throw her athletic legs high in the air screaming and cheering for Marcus who was a starter on the freshman football team. Marcus scored in almost every game. Louis lost interest in football and was rarely seen in the weight room. He spent game time mostly on the end of the bench watching from the sidelines.

Over time, the gossip column about Marcus taking Louis' girlfriend became old news. Campus life was slowly getting back to normal. Louis regained his focus in school and started going back to the weight room. Then one day, during sixth period, Louis had a setback.

The students in Louis' sixth period class were normally rambunctious and rowdy after lunch. On this day, they simply refused to settle down. Louis was also talking and goofing around. In a desperate attempt to settle down the class, their teacher Mr. Boston singled out Louis and said, "You all need to settle down. And Louis, you don't need to talk at all. You can't even keep a girlfriend."

The entire class erupted in laughter. Students fell out of their seats laughing hysterically. Louis folded his arms on his desk and covered his face in shame. Tears rolled down his face. He was so embarrassed. The public humiliation was unbearable. Louis was now the butt of every joke on campus from the lunchroom to the teachers' lounge. Freshman Marcus Thomas had claimed the prettiest girl on campus by stealing her away from a popular sophomore on the varsity team who called himself The Ambassador. Louis was no longer the self-proclaimed campus ambassador. He was no longer the boyfriend of the prettiest girl on campus. Instead, now Louis was the butt of every joke on campus. Louis was the joke on the front-page news in the school gossip column, and Marcie and Marcus were the 'Cutest Couple' in the school yearbook.

Garey High School was a dreadful place for Louis. If it were not for the support of his two friends, Stanley Bibbs and Gary Lett, Louis would have dropped out of high school altogether. Louis' buddies were sympathetic. During lunch, the three of them sat together in the bleachers on the football field. They were as far away as possible from the crowd. Louis was visibly dejected. "I cannot believe your teacher would stoop so low and make such a rude and embarrassing remark in front of the entire class about a student!" Stanley started.

"Who does he think he is?" Gary added.

Stanley continued, "What goes on among students, if it does not concern class or interfere with class, is not the teacher's business. As a teacher, he should be ashamed of himself, and should be reported to the principal and reprimanded!"

"Don't worry", Gary added, "Marcie will be crawling back on her hands and knees begging for your forgiveness."

The words of encouragement from Louis' buddies had fallen on deaf ears. Louis had completely lost interest in school. The public humiliation and peer pressure were too much to bear. Louis had completely lost confidence in himself. His interest in school was gone, entirely.

"Hey! Let's go to the Grambling vs. Long Beach State football game at the L.A. Coliseum this upcoming Labor Day weekend," suggested Stanley. "Some of the prettiest girls in L.A. will surely be in attendance. We will have a blast!"

"That sounds like a plan!" Gary added. "Grambling will bring their world-famous marching band and powerhouse football team. Long Beach State will showcase Terry Metcalf, one of the best running backs in the country."

"Get your mind off Garey High School and Marcie, and let's have some real fun," insisted Stanley. The three agreed. They would go to the Grambling vs. Long Beach State game on Labor Day weekend.

Chapter 6

The Eye of The Tiger

Los Angeles is known for its terrible rush hour traffic. On Labor Day, it was horrendous. The freeway traffic was bumper to bumper. Once Louis and his friends exited the freeway, the streets were crowded with people. Grambling vs. Long Beach State was the hottest ticket in town. Vendors lined the sidewalks selling t-shirts, banners, chilidogs, and sodas. The atmosphere was electric. A row of buses was parked a few blocks down the street, not far from the stadium entrance.

Cheers from the crowd exploded as Grambling's band exited the buses in full uniform like rockstars. The band members unloaded their Instruments, tuned their horns, and secured their chin straps. Just that quick, Louis had forgotten about Garey High School. He had never seen so many people in an atmosphere buzzing with excitement and anticipation.

The band fell into formation as the drum majors blew their whistles. Grambling College Marching Band was in full formation for all of Los Angeles to see. It was their first time on the West Coast. Like a military platoon ready to battle on foreign soil, the high-stepping Grambling Tigers were ready to perform. They first played “Can’t Get Enough” by R&B recording artist Barry White. The crowd went wild!

Singing and dancing commenced as far as the eye could see. Hips were shaking as people did the cha-cha in the streets just a few blocks away from the stadium entrance. A switch had turned on and the game hadn’t even started. The energy and festivities from the streets poured into the stadium. Even the bleachers seemed to be rocking to the beat of Grambling’s Marching Band. The game was good, but the half- time show was spectacular. L.A. got a taste of what Historically Black Colleges have always known: The real attraction of a football game is not during regulation time. The true battle happens at half time when the band steps onto the field. Grambling did not disappoint!

Louis never felt so much positive energy. He had never seen so many beautiful girls and smiling faces. As a sophomore, Louis had not given much thought to where he wanted to go to college. He only thought about Marcie, football, and lifting weights. Now, a new joy of life thrilled him. He knew exactly where he wanted to attend college. Louis wanted to go to Grambling College!

***

The day after Labor Day, Louis ran to school. He ran past the chatter of girls at the school entrance. He went straight into the main office hoping to see his counselor, Mrs. Gregoire. Her door was open, and she was available.

“Good morning Mrs. Gregoire. I want to go to college... Grambling College. What do I have to do?”

She pointed to a bookshelf full of reference books arranged in alphabetical order and said, “Look under L.”

Louis inquired, “Why L?”

"Because Grambling is in the state of Louisiana," Mrs. Gregoire replied.

Louis had to check the map. He had no idea how far away Grambling College was from California. It didn't matter to him. Louis' mind was set.

"First, you need to research and write down the school's address." Louis quickly scanned the pages in the book-marked L, inside he located Grambling College.

"Got it!" he exclaimed. The adrenalin was still flowing from Saturday's thrilling game and half-time performance.

"Now, write this down," Mrs. Gregoire instructed. Louis jotted down Mrs. Gregoire's statement verbatim:

To Whom It May Concern,

My name is Louis Sheppard. I am a student at Garey High School in Pomona, California. I would very much like to attend Grambling College. Please send me an application for admission and all financial aid forms.

Mrs. Gregoire reminded Louis, "Don't expect anything back until the end of your junior year. You are only a sophomore."

Louis was determined to get out of high school. He was annoyed with the daily girls' chatter and teammates' heckling. After Saturday's game, Grambling College was his college choice.

Several weeks passed. Louis received a letter in the mail. It was from Grambling College. The application had arrived. Louis was excited! On Monday morning, Louis went directly to Mrs. Gregoire's office. "Good morning Mrs. Gregoire. Guess what? I received the application for admission from Grambling College in the mail yesterday. What do I do now?" he inquired.

"Congratulations!" said Mrs. Gregoire. Then she instructed him to read everything carefully, twice if necessary. "This is only an information packet from the Grambling Admissions Office. Let's not get too excited," she said. "Remember Louis, you are only a second-semester sophomore. You have time. No need to rush in completing the application," she advised.

Louis carefully read Grambling's information packet. He carefully read it twice. Grambling's application process required a copy of official transcripts, two letters of recommendation, and Scholastic Aptitude Test (SAT) scores.

Going against the better judgment of his counselor, Louis decided to fill out the application for admission immediately. On the application, Louis marked his status as a junior at Garey High School, not a sophomore. Louis scheduled the SAT and requested transcripts to be sent to Grambling's Office of Admissions. He requested his two letters of recommendations from his favorite teachers. Then he completed and mailed the application with the letters of recommendation to Grambling. He did this all under the pretense that he was a junior. Now, it was a waiting game.

Louis went to school and stayed in the weight room preparing for the upcoming football season. The application he mailed was far from his mind. Marcie and Marcus were also in his rear-view mirror. His sophomore year was nearly over when he received another letter in the mail postmarked from Grambling College. He went directly to Mrs. Gregoire's office and sat down. Louis handed the letter to Mrs. Gregoire. She saw the letter was still sealed and postmarked the Grambling College Office of Admission. Mrs. Gregoire slowly opened her top desk door. She took out her letter opener and proceeded to open the envelope. Mrs. Gregoire read the letter to herself. As she read the letter, there was no expression on her face indicating whether the letter was a rejection or acceptance notification. She slowly raised her head, cleared her throat, and read the letter aloud.

Dear Louis Sheppard,

Congratulations!

You have been accepted to Grambling College for the Fall term. This letter of acceptance is pending the receipt of your official SAT scores and official transcript. These documents are required for official admission. Official Transcripts and SAT scores are sent directly to our Office of Admissions.

Again, congratulations.

Louis felt chills throughout his body as Mrs. Gregoire read aloud.

Two weeks passed. Louis received another letter postmarked from Grambling College Office of Admissions. The Grambling Admissions Office had received Louis' SAT scores and his official transcript from Garey High School's records office. His application for admission at Grambling College was officially complete. Congratulations were now in order.

Chapter 7

The Journey of a Thousand Miles

Louis was anxious to share the news with his parents. Until that moment, Louis had never revealed his mission. He knew how much they emphasized the importance of education. Although they never earned a high school diploma, they were sticklers about education.

Louis' mother earned a GED at the age of 35. She raised four children. She worked in a kitchen at a group home and then later as a cook at a local college. Blisters from splattering hot grease left bruises on her hands and arms. Yet, she never complained.

When Louis' father was in the fifth grade, he dropped out of school to help his mother. He later enlisted in the Armed Services. He became a Military Police Officer in a racially segregated Army. After an honorable discharge from the military, he worked in construction. He was always a no-nonsense dad who was revered throughout the city as a stern man with zero tolerance for laziness. His military training was evident in his parenting style and the whole neighborhood knew it, especially Louis' buddy Stanley who wrote this poem:

My Dead Old Pad

It was during the summer of '72,

The pad was depressing because there was nothing to do.

When I get up and finish dressing, I go play basketball.

When I come home, Pops is upset because Stan just called.

After coming home, from shooting baskets,

I come home to this dead old casket.

Listen to lectures while eating dinner.

Eat up the lecture and not the food.

Maybe that is why I am getting thinner.

And with the lecture, maybe that is why I am a mixed-up dude.

Being yelled at with a shout and scream,

I always keep hoping this was a dream.

Hell is living with Dad.

324 Drifton, my dead old pad.

Stanley was not only a gifted speaker, but also an excellent writer. His poem, "My Dead Old Pad", was published in the school newspaper, where it gained campus-wide notoriety and earned him high marks in his creative writing class. The poem captured the essence of Louis' teenage years nearly perfectly. Pops ran his household like a boot camp. His military police experience was in full effect in the Sheppard household. Louis' sanity came from being outdoors, playing football or lifting weights.

Chores were assigned regularly. Cutting the lawn, pulling weeds, washing the car every Saturday, and even changing the oil and filter in both parents' cars were routine chores for Louis and

Michael. Sisters Francine and Clarice had house chores, too. They washed clothes, vacuumed the house, polished furniture, and learned to cook under the watchful eye of Mom. At the end of every dinner, dishes were washed, and nothing was left in the sink to dry. Trash was emptied and the floors were swept. The kitchen was spotless. The Sheppard household was structured and disciplined. Reluctance to work was simply unacceptable.

Neither parent knew Louis was particularly interested in attending college. They knew of Louis' interest in Marcie. They had both grown fond of Marcie. However, they had no idea he was seriously considering college, especially since he was only a sophomore. Louis' mother knew he was in the second semester of his sophomore year with decent grades. She also noticed Louis was suddenly focused on his studies.

Yet, in the celebration of Louis' acceptance, they learned that his losing Marcie caused an embarrassment for Louis that nearly extinguished his interest in school. They had no idea attending a college football game would rekindle his fire and focus on school, graduation, academic excellence and finally college. They were proud of Louis' ability to change his suffering into success. A huge celebration was had by all!

***

Louis couldn't wait to share the news with his buddies! "Guess what?" Louis announced during lunchtime with Stanley and Gary in the bleachers. "I have been accepted to Grambling college!"

"How are you going to college when you haven't even graduated from high school?" asked Stanley. "You are such a jokester. Who would accept a student who has only completed their sophomore year in high school into college?"

"Think what you want," Louis snapped back. "I am going to Grambling College next Fall. I don't care what you say or what you think."

Louis was agitated by his buddy's sarcastic response. Louis fired back with a quote from the great Chinese philosopher Lao Tzu, "The journey of a thousand miles begins with a single step."

Stanley and Gary were both silent. Deep inside Louis knew he had no choice. Either he could graduate from high school early or succumb to the hurtful gossip rapidly eroding his self-esteem. Deep inside Louis knew finishing high school early was better than the humiliation he suffered at the hands of his high school peers.

"Well, if you have been accepted to Grambling," said Gary, "that is cause for celebration. There is a party tomorrow night at Scotty's house. Let's go and celebrate!"

The following night, the three squeezed into Gary's blue Volkswagen. They decided to dine at a local Mexican Restaurant. They ordered tacos and Mexican-style chicken soup with crackers. With bellies full, they were ready to party. The street was lined with cars. Strobe lights flashed through the front window and the music was blaring.

When Louis, Gary, and Stanley entered Scotty's house, it was packed with people dancing. The DJ had the house rocking. Louis asked for directions to the washroom. He was in the washroom less than a minute when a tap came at the door. It was Gary. "Hey man, your girl Marcie and Marcus just entered the party," warned Gary. Louis panicked. He finally understood the word his English teacher often used, claustrophobic – an irrational fear of confined places. Louis felt trapped. There was no way he was going to party with Marcie and his nemesis, Marcus. Louis started sweating profusely. He imagined exiting the washroom to the heckling of girls in the party. Many of his teammates were also present at the party. They would surely chime in and create an atmosphere too humiliating for Louis to endure. He had only one escape route, the washroom window. Louis managed to balance himself on top of the toilet seat. He climbed out the window. He dropped down into Scotty's backyard like Spiderman. Louis hopped over Scotty's fence and quickly left the party. Louis ran all the way home and went straight to his bedroom. He locked his bedroom door, turned on his desk lamp, and began working on a science project that was due on Monday. This was Louis' last assignment before he was scheduled to officially withdraw from Garey High School.

***

The following week, Louis returned to his neighborhood school, San Dimas High School in the Bonita Unified School District. This was all a part of fulfilling the mission of graduating in time to start Grambling in the Fall.

Louis needed a faster way to earn high school credits. Thanks to San Dimas High's Pre-Freshman summer school, Louis had already earned ten credits and started high school ahead of the game. Now, when he returned to San Dimas High, he found that it had converted to a trimester system with 240 credits required for graduation. In the next two trimesters at San Dimas High School, Louis earned credits equivalent to a full year of learning at Garey High School.

Garey High School was Louis' primary motivator. Louis may have left behind the ridicule and shame he faced at Garey High, but the heartache of losing Marcie was his ever-present shadow. Like a shadow, the heartache walked with Louis everywhere he went growing bigger then smaller then bigger again with each passing hour. He would never want this pain for anyone he loved.

Chapter 8

Mountains to Climb

One Saturday afternoon. Louis awakened to the sounds of screams in the next room. His mother was consoling his older sister Francine. It was hard to imagine what could be wrong with Francine. Francine had just enrolled in her first year at the University of Southern California. She was the smartest of the siblings with a promising future.

Francine was devastated. She had just lost her first-born child. The baby girl was only four months old. The entire house was in mourning. Louis, who was always looking for a reason to joke, found himself helpless when faced with the loss of a child. Louis knew the heartache of losing someone you love. He knew the void it left in the pit of your stomach. He knew how the pain makes you implode leaving you with the impossible task of picking up a million shards of your shattered self. He knew how heartache becomes a shadow and is always there. This time, however, Louis knew his loss of Marcie was minuscule compared to Francine's pain and suffering over losing her baby girl.

Weeks later, the house appeared to return to normalcy. Then there was sobbing again coming from Francine's room. Pops rushed into the room to inquire. He was concerned that his daughter was having a relapse over her baby's death.

"What's wrong?" Pops asked in a delicate concerned tone.

Francine muttered through her sobs, "Charles' younger brother Demmie has been making fun of me losing the baby." Francine's eyes were swollen with tears. She turned away from Mom who was sitting bedside. Francine buried her face in her pillow.

Louis overheard the reason why his sister was crying and who was to blame. He was furious! Louis knew all too well how it felt to be ridiculed and shamed over losing someone you love. Louis may have had to endure it for himself without retort, but he wasn't going to let his sister's nemesis go without retribution! Louis was known to be hot-tempered, especially when it comes to defending his family. This time he had his sights set on Demmie.

Louis did not know Charles's younger brother Demmie, but he did know Charles. Charles was the father of Francine's deceased baby girl. For some odd reason, his younger brother Demmie thought the loss of a child was funny. Louis felt personally offended. His sister had lost a child. He had lost a niece. His parents had lost a grandchild.

Louis knew the high school that Demmie attended. Demmie attended Ganesha High School in Pomona. Between Louis' home and Ganesha High School sat Frank G. Bonelli Regional Park and the Interstate 10 freeway.

One foggy morning on the way to school, hotheaded Louis began to boil with anger. Instead of walking to San Dimas High, Louis decided to take a dangerous detour. Louis' anger carried him over the hills of Frank G. Bonelli Regional Park. He journeyed on a 30-minute trek over Bonelli Park's last and highest hill of thorny cacti. It looked like a mountain to Louis. He passed slithering snakes and walked beyond the howls of coyotes. On the other side of this mountain, Louis faced the early morning traffic on the Interstate 10 freeway.

The foggy morning produced poor visibility. Louis was a daredevil. He timed his freeway crossing with an agility that took him safely to the other side of the freeway. Now, the only thing separating Louis from the main campus of Ganesha High School was a 10-foot chain-link fence and the school's football field. Louis scaled the fence, jumped down halfway on the other side and landed on the ground, like Spiderman. His athleticism came in handy. His adrenaline was still high from reflecting on the cries of his mother and sister over Demmie making fun of the death of Louis' four-month-old niece. Despite Louis' dangerous trek to the campus, he still had enough fuel in his tank to search for and confront Demmie who thought it was funny that Francine lost her first-born child.

Louis calmly approached the quad area of the main campus. Students were gathering before school eating breakfast near the snack bar. Louis calmly approached the first person he saw. "Excuse me. Do you happen to know a boy named Demmie?" Louis asked, trying to sound like he was not looking for trouble.

"Yes," a boy answered, then pointed to a group of boys nearby.

"Thank you," Louis said. Then like a tiger, he carefully approached the group of boys and asked, "Is your name Demmie?

"Who wants to know?" The boy retorted. Demmie was slender in size. He was the same height and age as Louis. Demmie, however, was not athletically built like Louis.

Louis responded, "My name is Louis. I am Francine's brother. I live in San Dimas, on the other side of that mountain," Louis said pointing in the direction of his treacherous journey. "I came here to let you know, if you have something smart to say about my sister losing her baby, you had better stop right now or you can deal with me right here and now." Louis' body language told of his anger and willingness to fight. The crowd began to back away anticipating a confrontation between Louis and Demmie.

"That wasn't me," Demmie pleaded.

"Word has it, it was you?" Louis said, taking a step closer positioning himself in a combat stance.

Demi continued to deny any wrongdoing, retreating from a sure and physical confrontation with Louis.

"Don't let me have to climb over that mountain again," Louis threatened, with his fist ready to strike.

Luckily the arrival bell sounded to start school. Most of the students in the quad disappeared. Louis got one last intimidating stare into the eyes of Demi. Dem's expression was a sign of guilt. Louis was satisfied he had made his point. He scampered back across the football field. He hopped the fence and dodged the morning freeway traffic again. Then Louis climbed back up the mountain and down the other side. After making his way back through Bonelli Park, Louis was finally on his way to his designated high school, hot -tempered and still angry.

***

There was no doubt Louis kept track of his family. There was also no doubt Louis kept track of his earned high school credits regardless of the school. He kept track when he was at Garey High which is easy to do when you are an office aide. Now, he was really keeping track since his return to San Dimas High. Louis requested an unofficial copy of his transcript from San Dimas High's records office. He scheduled an appointment with his counselor for a grad check.

After the grad check, Louis discovered he was closer to finishing high school if he was in a district that only required 220 credits to graduate. He knew he had to leave San Dimas High School at the end of the second trimester. Louis returned to Pomona Unified School District's semester system. Only this time, he enrolled in Pomona High school, the cross-town rival of Garey High.

At Pomona High, a full daily schedule included five classes. However, early graduates or credit deficient students could take an additional class known as the sixth period. Louis took advantage of this opportunity and enrolled in a six-period class. He even set his sights on extracurricular activities.

During the enrollment process, Louis learned that Pomona High School had just assembled a weightlifting team. The team had an upcoming league-wide weightlifting competition. Pomona was slated to enter. Louis was excited and anxious to join the team.

His hopes of competing were nearly derailed when he fractured his wrist horseplaying. He was confined to a cast for six weeks and forbidden to lift weights, doctor's orders. All he could do was sit idly by in the weight room watching the guys preparing for the competition.

Even in a cast and against doctor's orders, Louis secretly managed to do some exercises. In the privacy of his bedroom, he would do push-ups late at night before bed and early in the morning before going to school. He knew he could not compete at a high level if he remained in a cast the entire six weeks. Louis was impatient. Eventually, he removed the cast altogether ahead of schedule, complaining of itching.

Miraculously, when he did remove the cast, his hand was healed. His left hand and arm were noticeably smaller than before. With a week of daily lifting, his strength improved.

After class each day, Louis was in the weight room working out. This was his moment to shine. This was his moment to shed the image of being that loser he left behind at Garey High School. What better place than the weight room potentially competing against his now cross-town rival.

On the very day of the competition, Louis was fully confident he was ready. All the competitors weighed in. Louis had planned to compete in the 145lbs weight class. When he stepped on the scale, the judge announced he was three pounds overweight and would have to compete in a higher weight division. Louis was confident he would win in the 145lbs weight division, but less certain he would even place in a higher weight division.

The head judge announced all competitors were allowed a final weigh-in before the competition, if necessary. Louis knew he needed to shed 3 pounds. The only way he knew how to lose the weight was to run. He was gifted with a full body plastic sweatsuit by an official for such an occasion. Louis dashed out of the gymnasium down the hill onto the track below and started running. He ran for nearly 25 minutes in the sweltering heat determined to make weight and compete in the 145lbs weight class. He sweated profusely for 25 minutes, running before the final weigh-in.

When the final weigh-in was announced, Louis stripped down to his boxers, and stepped onto the scale. He took a deep breath. The scale tipped in his favor. He weighed in at exactly 145lbs. Louis exhaled in relief. He climbed to the top of the bleachers and waited for the competition to start.

Three hours later, the competition was finally over. Louis place 1st in the 145lbs division.

His self-esteem was restored. His confidence was back. He proudly walked the campus still wearing his blue and gold varsity letterman's jacket from Garey High School.

Monday morning following the competition, his name along with other successful competitors were announced over the intercom. Even as a new incoming transfer student wearing a rival letterman jacket, Louis was confident on the campus of his soon-to-be alma mater, Pomona High School, Home of the Red Devils.

***

One week before graduation, Louis scheduled a credit check with his counselor. He discovered he was short 2.5 credits in American Government. One semester of American government was a graduation requirement. Louis was distraught and agitated.

"What can I do?" he pleaded. "I have been to three schools in one school year trying to graduate early."

"Don't worry. You are only a junior. You are far ahead and will graduate over the summer or mid-semester of your senior year," the counselor said.

"That is too late." He presented his counselor with the letter of acceptance from Grambling's Admission office. The counselor was surprised.

"How did you manage to accumulate 219.5 credits before the end of your junior year?" she asked. "I will talk to Mr. Phillips, the Adult School Principal, and see if under these circumstances, you can be admitted earning 2.5 credits. This will be a first if he approves, especially since you are not an adult. The minimum age requirement to attend Adult School is 18 years. You are 17 years of age requesting permission to attend adult school. I am only your counselor. The principal here at Pomona is the only person who can speak on your behalf. I can only verify that you are a transfer student in good standing needing 2.5 credits to graduate. Come back later this afternoon, I will talk to the principal. As your counselor, the best I can do is show the principal your acceptance letter and transcript, that should help."

A few days later, Louis was called into the counselor's office. She immediately called Pomona Adult School and said, "May I speak to Mr. Phillips... Good afternoon, Sir, I have a student in my office, who would like to speak to you. His name is Louis Sheppard." With that, she handed the phone to Louis.

Mr. Phillips was aware of Louis' situation. As soon as Louis said hello, Mr. Phillips said, "Good morning, Mr. Sheppard. I am fully aware of your credit deficiency dilemma. I have seen your acceptance letter to Grambling College for this upcoming Fall semester. It is my understanding; you need credits to fulfill your high school graduation requirements.

"Yes Sir," replied Louis. Louis was holding his breath; not sure if Mr. Phillips would approve his request.

Mr. Phillips continued, "Congratulations young man. I am granting you special permission to enroll here at Pomona Adult school. See you Monday at 4 pm. And don't be late, Sir."

Louis breathed a sigh of relief and said, "Thank you Sir." He was nearly in tears. Louis was getting closer to completing his mission of graduating by the end of his junior year.

After taking two finals exams at Pomona High on Monday, Louis took a bus downtown to Pomona Adult School. When he checked in at the front counter, the clerk directed him to have a seat in an empty classroom across the hall. Minutes later, he was given a pamphlet to read on American Government. He carefully read the pamphlet with the weight of his pending graduation hanging in the balance. When Louis finished, he went to the front counter where the clerk handed him a scantron test and a #2 pencil. Over several hours, he was given several more pamphlets and scantron tests. Louis had to retain half of a semester amount of American Government. The tests were intense. Finally, he was summoned to the front counter where he received an envelope. Inside the envelope was a letter on Pomona Adult School letterhead with one sentence that read:

"Congratulations, you have earned 2.5 credits in American Government."

Louis was elated! He had done it! Mission accomplished! Louis had finally fulfilled his high school graduation requirements!

The next day, Louis ran to the front office, barged into the counselor's office unannounced, and breathlessly shared the good news. "I got it done," he blurted out. "I have earned the 2.5 credits in American Government in one day." Louis was beaming with joy.

"Calm down young man and please, have a seat," said the counselor. "You see that stack of unopened boxes in the corner next to the file cabinet on the floor?" she asked. "Those boxes contain the graduation programs, just delivered to my office this morning. The names of all the students scheduled to graduate are printed in the program. Unfortunately, your name is not in the program."

"What?" exclaimed Louis with genuine surprise. Louis wanted to cry. He slumped down in the high-backed chair directly across from the counselor. "I promised you, I was going to finish," he pleaded.

"Senior Grad check was held before you transferred to Pomona High. We can only calculate credits earned, not credits promised to earn," replied the counselor.

Louis was speechless from the disappointing news. After all the work he had done and schools he had attended, Louis would not be allowed to graduate this year. Even though he had met all the graduation requirements, Louis' name was not printed in the official graduation program.

"Plus," added the counselor, "there are no more cap and gowns. Cap and gowns were pre-ordered and distributed to this year's graduating class last week. Even if you were allowed to participate in the commencement ceremony, you would not have a cap and gown."

Louis was dejected. He had done everything he knew how to do, but still failed. Louis slowly raised his head, stood up and turned to leave the counselor's office.

"Just one minute," the counselor suddenly remembered, "I almost forgot. We do have a graduating senior who has not taken his last final examination. If he passes his examination, he will graduate. If he does not, he will not graduate. The student in question is scheduled to take his examination this afternoon. Come back to my office tomorrow," said the counselor, "I will know the outcome."

That night after dinner, Louis went to his room. He knelt quietly beside his bed and prayed. The following day, an extra cap and gown were available. They were folded nice and neat on top of the counselor's desk. Louis breathed another sigh of relief. He hurriedly tried on the cap. Neither the cap nor gown fit. The cap and gown were two sizes larger than needed. The cap was an extra-large and practically covered Louis' head and eyes. The gown was also too big. It nearly dragged on the ground and its sleeves covered Louis' arms and his hands. Louis had to manage. It was the only cap and gown available. The good news was Louis would be participating in tomorrow's commencement as the only underclassman to become a graduating senior within one school year! If there was a dictionary entry for the phrase: I can do anything I put my mind to, Louis' picture would be there as the example!

Chapter 9

Commencement

Louis decided to get a fresh haircut. To be even more spectacular, on such a special occasion, Louis decided to dye his hair black. Even though his hair was already black, he wanted it jet black, for graduation. Louis had no prior knowledge of how to administer hair dye. He knew nothing of the steps or procedures. He went to the local store, purchased hair dye, and went straight to the washroom at home to squeeze the dye onto his hair. Louis didn't even bother to read the instructions. The only thing on his mind was tomorrow's graduation.

After several minutes hovering over the sink, he rinsed his hair with water. When he finished rinsing his hair, the strangest thing happened. The palms of Louis' hands were completely black. The edges of his ears were black, and his neck was dyed black. He was a mess with a nice haircut.

Louis couldn't do anything about his dye debacle. He could, however, make sure he wasn't a mess with a nice haircut during the ceremony. He had some catching up to do. Graduation rehearsal was crucial. Since Louis was not scheduled to graduate, he had not been called out of class to participate in graduation rehearsals. He was clueless on where and when to line up for commencement. He did not know the graduating class would be lining up in alphabetical order and marching in to the tune, "Pomp and Circumstance." He did not know what side the tassel turns at the end of the ceremony. What he did know was where the commencement ceremony was being held. The ceremony would be held at the Pomona County Fair Grounds, at the racetrack.

By the time Louis and his parents arrived at Pomona Fairground, the parking lot was jammed full. In the distance, he could barely hear "Pomp and Circumstance" playing. He knew the approximate time to be at graduation, but not the exact time. Realizing he was tardy, he started to trot with quickness. The commencement ceremony had barely begun. The stadium was colorful. Balloons swayed in the morning breeze. Cameras were flashing and children were hoisted onto the shoulders of their parents.

A red and white banner stretched across the length of the stage read Congratulations Class of '73. The atmosphere was festive. Names were being called, the procession was moving to the familiar tune of "Pomp and Circumstance." When commencement began, Louis was not in the procession. He was not even in the stadium. He darted from graduate to graduate asking their last name to know exactly where he belonged. Meanwhile, the line was moving. A few graduates before the stage steps, Louis finally found his proper place in line. He was breathing heavily from dashing through the line. By the time he was a few steps away from the steps of the stage, he had regained his composure. He was ready for the next step. A piece of paper was handed to the counselor announcing the names of the graduates.

"Louis Sheppard," the counselor finally called. Louis proudly received his diploma, unknowingly in the wrong hand, and slowly walked across the stage shaking hands with the principal and District Superintendent along the way.

"Congratulations, son," whispered the principal proudly, "You did it. You are a high school graduate."

"Thank you, Sir," Louis said with a smile.

No one was happier on graduation day than his parents and friends who were present in the audience. Louis paused for a moment for photos as he crossed the stage, then turned his smile to the audience.

Out of the sea of people, there were only two people he recognized. The first person of course was Mom. Louis' mother wore her red and white dress. She had a handkerchief in her hand as tears streamed down her cheeks. Louis saw she was gleaming with pride to see her baby son graduate. Just behind Mom's shoulder in the next row, he saw the second familiar face. This face would forever make him smile. This face caused him joy and pain.

Was it true? Was it Marcie? How did she know? He wondered.

Marcie was wearing the colors of her alma mater, blue and gold. She was looking as beautiful as ever. She flashed that signature dimpled smile, waved, and winked at Louis all at once. His heart skipped a beat. He had not seen Marcie in months; not since he had withdrawn from Garey High School.

As he made his way through fellow graduates, Louis finally reached his family and friends. Pops proudly shook Louis' hand. His friends high-fived Louis. Then Louis hugged his mother and presented her with his diploma.

"This is for you Mom," he said.

Tears streaming down her face, "I am so proud of you, Son. You fulfilled your dream and mind too, all at the same time." Standing in the row just behind his mother, was Marcie. He proudly gave Marcie his graduation cap.

"Thank you for coming, Marcie. Had it not been for you, I would not be standing here today. You are my motivator, inspirator and reason to complete high school." Louis and Marcie took several photos together. She handed him a graduation gift in a bag. Then walked away.

"Goodbye, my love," Louis said as he watched Marcie disappear into the crowd.

Once in the car, Louis hurriedly opened Marcie's gift. It was in a black gift bag with gold streamers. To Louis' surprise, Marcie's gift was a Black and Gold jersey. On the front it read, Grambling College.

Louis and Stanley celebrated graduation by riding out to Venice Beach. They stopped along the way at a burger stand. They ordered burgers, fries, and strawberry milkshakes. At the beach, Louis and Stan laid in the warm sand with their arms positioned triumphantly behind their heads, staring up into the blue sky. They watched the seagulls dive into the ocean. Louis was relieved. He thought of the graduation festivities and how proud his parents were to see him awarded his diploma. What he reflected on most was seeing Marcie. How did she know he was graduating?

Even with the hours-long, rush hour traffic of Los Angeles, they made it home before nightfall. As the day turned to night, Louis wondered why he could not bury the past and live in the present the way he buried his toes in the sand. He decided to close the Marcie chapter. It was time to move on with his life.

Chapter 10

Road Trip

Pop was beaming with pride when his son graduated. He boasted about his son going to college a year early. To show how excited he was, instead of putting his son on a bus to travel to college, Pops decided to drive him to Louisiana himself. Mom agreed. She thought it was an excellent idea. Pops and Louis needed to spend quality time together as father and son before Louis officially stepped out on his own.

To celebrate his success, Mom made Louis' favorite dessert, homemade banana pudding with meringue on top. Mom made the best banana pudding! She made it with crunchy vanilla wafers baked golden from the oven. "I love you, son. You know I never graduated from high school. I dropped out of school, fell in love, and got married at the age of seventeen. I barely learned how to read at age thirty-five. The world is rough when you do not have an education," she declared, "and rougher when you are far from home in a strange place without a support system." Mom continued to drop nuggets along the way on how to navigate problematic personal relationships.

Louis listened and reflected on the challenges he had faced throughout his life. School was one of those challenges. Louis learned how to read confidently in the fifth grade. Prior to that, when his teacher asked students to read aloud, Louis avoided the task. When he knew he was about to be called on to read, he would raise his hand to go to the restroom. Louis would sit on the toilet in a closed bathroom stall long enough to be certain the oral reading section was over. He knew sooner or later the teacher would ask him to read and the whole class would realize that he stumbled over simple words, words every fifth grader should phonetically pronounce with ease. Frustrated and developing an early case of anxiety, Louis realized he needed help with his reading.

Louis went home, unzipped his backpack, and took out his thick World Civilization textbook. He took it to his mother and said, "Mom, can you read a few pages about The Trojan Horse from the book 'The Iliad and The Odyssey'? This story is read aloud daily in class."

Louis desperately wanted to understand the text. He wanted to know the words and pronounce each one properly.

"Sure Son," Mom said, smiling confidently. Since she dropped out of school and did not have a formal education, Mom suspected Louis thought she could not read. Listening to his mother read aloud sounded like music to Louis' ears. He finally understood the Trojan Horse. Achilles and Agamemnon became his favorite characters in the story. Words, initially he would not dare to pronounce, now flowed from Mom's lips like a sweet song. WOW! His mother was an excellent reader.

"Before I dropped out of school, reading was my best subject," Mom admitted. "Now you read Son."

Mom insisted while moving closer and turning the book more in Louis' direction. At that moment, she realized her son needed serious help with reading. From that day forward, Louis read aloud to his mother for thirty minutes each day. Soon, he was reading confidently, pronouncing words phonetically. He no longer had an urge to go to the restroom during oral reading time in class.

"Thank you, Mom, for being my best teacher. You taught me how to read. Through patience and love, I learned to read for comprehension and enjoyment."

"I picked the right son," she smiled.

With this memory and Mom's words of advice, Louis knew he could face and triumph over any challenge life would bring his way. He packed his bags and invited his good friend Stan to ride along on the cross-country trip to Grambling.

Pops liked Stan. Stan was talkative, comical, and witty. He was a good driver and would be good company on a three-day road trip.

Before leaving California, Pops decided to gift his son with a new wardrobe. Pops went downtown to the L.A. Garment District to buy school clothes for Louis. Pops purchased several colorful shirts, undershirts, socks, jeans and two pairs of dress shoes. Louis was outfitted as a college student.

Together, Pops, Stan and Louis set out on the road to Louisiana in the white Dodge camper, also known as the family truck. The truck had a bench seat which allowed the three occupants to sit side by side. They would take turns driving. Switching drivers allowed them to cover more miles and each of them more time to sleep. The journey from California to Louisiana was long and the hardships in the desert were many.

There were many fond memories on the three-day road trip. None more memorable than when Louis openly decided to disobey his father's instructions. Louis grew distressed as the trip wore on and they were forced to listen to Pop's constant fussing and complaining. Louis and Stan were instructed, when it was their turn to drive, to stay under the speed limit: 65 miles per hour, regardless of the flow of the traffic. Pops was extra cautious, especially since Louis only had a driver's permit. Pops was taking a chance allowing his son to drive out of state without a driver's license. Nonetheless, with Louis behind the wheel, Pops dozed off in the passenger seat with his head leaning against the passenger window snoring. Louis decided to put his foot on the accelerator defying his Pop, driving faster than the Texas speed limit.

"You had better slow down," advised Stan who sat in the middle between Louis and Pops. Louis ignored his friend's advice and started driving even faster. Louis changed lanes excessively. He was having fun speeding without using the land change indicator. Suddenly, there was a gust of high winds. Tumbleweeds and debris swirled across the Interstate affecting visibility and causing Louis to swerve. Pops woke up. The abrupt shift in the camper startled Pops. He was furious! When he glanced over and saw Louis was driving faster than the speed limit and faster than instructed, Pops demanded, "Slow down boy! You are going to get us killed!"

Louis ignored the directive. With his wooden cane, Pops forcefully reached over Stan to knock Louis' foot off the accelerator pedal. In doing so, Pops hit Stan on his kneecap. Stan flinched in pain. From his grimacing facial expression, Louis knew his friend was hurt. "You alright?" Louis asked Stanley.

Pops took offense to his son consoling Stan, while still ignoring the directive to slowdown. "Slow down, Boy!!!" Pops yelled.

Louis gradually reduced his speed but was still driving faster than the speed limit. Pops was annoyed and said, "Pull over boy. I'll drive".

Louis was angry. His brain had overheated and blown a fuse. It is really frightening for a 17-year-old boy to confront a grownup, especially when that grownup was Pops. "We were supposed to share driving responsibilities on this road trip, but all you have been doing is sleeping. I thought you were going to teach us something about how to navigate and maneuver safely around 18-wheelers, and U-Haul trucks on the open highway. Instead, you are sightseeing, eating chips and snoring. Louis continued jabbing away at the mouth being argumentative with Pops. "You have taught us nothing. The only time you communicate with us is when you wake up, chastising us for driving too fast." Louis was certain his grievance was heard, and he had won the argument.

Pops was listening intensely to his son who sounded much like himself when angry.

Deep down, Louis had the utmost respect for his father. They just happened to be so much alike. Today, none of that mattered. Today, their eyes met like two fighters in a boxing ring. "Get out Boy. Pull over and get out," Pops insisted.

Louis reacted, slammed his foot on the brake in the middle of the Interstate sending Stan and Pops headfirst towards the dashboard. They all had to brace themselves against what could have been a serious accident. Pops lend over, with his walking cane and snatched the keys out the ignition in the middle of the interstate. The truck immediately slowed down.

"Pull over and get out of my truck!" Pops demanded a second time.

Louis pulled over to the shoulder of the road and gladly jumped out of the truck.

Louis looked at his friend and asked, "You comin'?"

Stanley had mixed feelings about getting out the truck, especially with a bruised knee. But he followed his friend and gingerly climbed out of the truck. Pops drove off, leaving no indication he was coming back.

In the scorching Texas sun, the boys walked and quarreled for miles.

"This is all your fault," Stan insisted. "Why do you always have to be argumentative with your Pops? I did not volunteer to come with you on a three-day road trip so I could be stranded in the desert."

"You did not have to get out," Louis responded abruptly.

"Your true friends accept you as you are," Stan replied, "even when your wires are crossed. And your wires are definitely crossed in how you interact with your Pops."

For miles the two boys walked and quarreled. Each hour the sun traveled across the sky, the boys walked slower and slower. The desert sun drained their energy with each step. Traffic was moving. Motorcycles, 18-wheelers, and U-hauls sped by. The boys could feel the blistering desert heat on their skin. The white camper was completely out of sight.

Hours later, Louis saw what appeared to be a vehicle in the distance. Louis wasn't sure if it was a mirage. It vaguely appeared to be a white camper parked along the side of the road.

"That looks like Pops' truck up ahead," Stan said. The boys were relieved.

"If it is," warned Stan, "don't say anything rude or disrespectful. If you do and Pops threatens to put us out again, you will be walking alone."

As the boys walked, Stan noticed movement in the dirt just off the roadside and it was moving in their direction. It was a Western diamondback rattlesnake, the most common and widespread snake in Texas. Its diamond-patterned skin, and black and white ringed tail camouflaged it in the dirt. Stan was frantic.

"Snake!" yelled Stan, "Run!"

The adrenaline rush gave the boys a burst of energy they did not know they had. Stan and Louis quickly took off running. No matter how hot the day or how tired their legs were from walking in the sweltering Texas heat, they ran to the white camper. To conserve the energy they had left, they ran without talking. As they approached the truck, sweaty and exhausted, Louis could vaguely see Pops' face in the side view mirror. When they got closer, close enough to grab the door, Pops leaped out of the truck in a rage.

"You trying to get us killed? You pull another stunt like that, boy, I will put you out again, turn this truck around, and head back to California. You can walk the rest of the way to Louisiana for all I care!" Pops was dead serious.

Stanley was also serious when he said, you will walk the Interstate alone, if you get put out again. Louis bit his lip but made no reply. They rode in silence until they reached Shreveport, Louisiana.

Shreveport was approximately sixty-five miles from Grambling which was less than an hour's drive away. It was Stan's turn to drive. He enjoyed driving cross country. He described it as a relaxing and therapeutic experience. Behind the wheel, Stan was mindful of tractor-trailer trucks, campers, U-Hauls, and motorcyclists who were driving faster than the speed limit. Stan was in a peaceful space in his own little world, almost in a trance, especially with his favorite R&B artist Earth, Wind & Fire playing on the radio.

Louis wanted to do something for his friend, especially since Louis had caused Stan so much grief. Louis glanced over with a smile, thankful for his dear friend who was always patient and supportive. Louis wanted to thank his friend verbally while Pops slept, but the more Louis considered this, the more difficult it seemed. So those words of thanks were left unsaid.

Louis was a youth himself, on his way to college. Louis was young and didn't have the maturity to express his feelings to his friend. He simply didn't know how to tell Stan; Man, I appreciate what you've done for me.

Pops was snoring and leaning once again against the window. The trip was nearly over. Stan slowed down and pulled over to the shoulder of the road.

"Pops, we are here."

Pops woke up, cleared his eyes, and said, "Pull over, I will take it from here."

Chapter 11

Tiger Town

Grambling was the next exit. After a three-day road trip, they had finally reached their destination. It was early Sunday morning. The town of Grambling was asleep. It was perfectly quiet except for the sound of crickets and frogs from the nearby ponds. The stars served as flashlights, shining bright in the heavens. Grambling was surrounded by a forest and swamplands. The towering trees parted to make way through the narrow road to the campus.

Grambling was also hot and humid. The air conditioner in the truck was faulty. So, it blew humid air through its dusty vents. There were no tissues or napkins in the glove compartment to wipe away the sweat. Their clothes were drenched, sticky and hot.

Pops drove into the campus on Main Street known as Tiger Village. Pops announced, "We made it boys. We finally made it to Grambling College!"

With fists pounding, they were elated.

The first landmark in the small town was Spivey's Fried Chicken and Restaurant, a favorite eatery of the Grambling students and local community. Mosquitoes and gnats were visible around the lamp post illuminating the modest restaurant. Pops parked just across the street from Spivey's. Even though it was still early morning, smoke was bellowing from the restaurant's chimney.

Music blaring from the jukebox inside the restaurant allowed Louis to inhale deeply and appreciate the moment. He had a vivid memory of often helping his mother prepare dinner. Sprinkling white flour, covered batter and a dash of seasoning on chicken just before it was dropped in the hot grease. Fried chicken and fries were his favorite as a youngster. The aroma of fried chicken from Spivey's Restaurant, the sounds of the music, was reminiscent of his childhood. He finally understood what his mother meant when she talked about being homesick.

Spivey's Chicken and Restaurant was Louis' first memorable landmark in Grambling.

The boys got out of the truck and proudly strolled the campus on foot. They walked past the Administration and Admissions buildings. They walked to the student cafeteria, student store, and the gymnasium. They finally came to the middle of the campus and rested on the bricks surrounding the fountain in the quad.

After their short and humid walk, the boys were exhausted. They were ready to go back to the camper and stretch out. In an instance, the boys dozed off to sleep, but not before Louis noticed several motor vehicles with campers just like theirs. Most had out of state license plates and were parked nearby. Young people were curiously milling around campus. He saw two young people with shirts identical to the one Marcie gave him for graduation. Freshman registration was going to be a big event.

***

A long line awaited Louis in front of the registration building. Louis, along with Stan, hurriedly took his place in line with other incoming freshmen and their parents. Pops observed from the truck. He was not interested in standing in line after a long cross-county road trip. He took a nap.

Two hours later, after standing in line in the sweltering Louisiana heat, Louis finally had his dormitory assignments and meal tickets. When Stan and Louis returned to the truck, Pops was awake with the windows rolled down, sightseeing.

"I am hungry," Pops blared. "Let's go get some chicken from Spivey's Restaurant."

The three decided to walk to Spivey's Restaurant and dine in. They ordered a family-size bucket of chicken wings, fries, and red soda water. The food was delicious! After a hardy lunch, registration, and dormitory assignment, Pops and Stan got in the car to head back to California.

"Goodbye my son. Do well in school. Make us proud," said Pops.

Louis asked, "You are not going to stay until tomorrow and see my dormitory, and help me unpack?"

"I have to get back. I have to go to work," Pops replied. "Besides, you are here safe and sound, just what your Mama wanted. You will find your way around. You will be fine," Pops said with confidence.

"Have fun my brother, and don't spend too much money," Stan said jokingly.

"See you on Christmas vacation," replied Louis. Louis stood solemnly with a heavy heart watching the white camper drive away. Things suddenly became surreal. There was no father to chastise him; no friend to encourage him to do the right thing. Louis turned and walked to his dorm alone with his luggage.

***

Louis was assigned to Crispus Attucks Hall, a freshmen dormitory facing the quad. When he entered Attucks Hall, he instantly felt the stifling heat in the lobby area. There was no air conditioning. Louis dragged his luggage in and sat down in the lobby. A tall, lanky unassuming guy was stretched out in the dorm front lobby, eating fried chicken and fries. He saw Louis enter the building and asked, "Can I help you?"

"Yes, my name is Louis. I am a freshman. I have been assigned to Attucks Hall," replied Louis.

"My name is Roy Lee Hadnott. I am a junior and I am the (RA) Resident Assistant for Attucks. If you need anything, I am here to assist you. Welcome to Grambling - Where Everybody is Somebody," he said with a cheerful smile. Roy's southern accent was heavy but pleasant. He had swagger, as he walked with confidence as though he owned Attucks Hall.

Roy escorted Louis to his assigned room, unlocked the door, turned, and began to walk away. Roy looked back over his shoulder and said, "If you need anything, I am just down the hall." Roy waved with his back turned and walked away to resume eating his lunch in the lobby.

Louis surveyed the room, placed his luggage on the floor and squatted with his hands clasped together in prayer. With his head bowed in silence, Louis was thankful. Finally, he was officially a Grambling Tiger.

When he opened his luggage, Louis was shocked. The school clothes Pops had purchased were cut into pieces. His old clothes, which were few, were untouched. Louis' mouth was gaping wide as moisture came to his eyes. He sat on the floor. With his back against the bed and his knees bent to his chest, Louis sat alone as tears rolled down. That is when he realized how angry Pops really was. Disappointed, Louis sat on the floor with his back against the bed in silence before he finally separated the shredded clothes from the old clothes in the open luggage. Exhausted, he finally stretched out on the tile floor next to his luggage, no blanket nor pillows and fell asleep.

The next morning, Louis reflected on the events of the road trip and how he was combative and disrespectful to Pops. He learned a valuable lesson - respect your elders, especially when it is your father. Words of wisdom from his mother reverberated in his mind when he awoke that morning. When you do good, good stars follow you, and when you do bad, bad stars follow you. The shouting match waged against Pops on the road trip had failed. Louis learned to respect his father once and for all.

He finally had the energy to unpack. He neatly folded his old shirts on the top closet shelf, hung up the only pair of blue jeans he had, and placed his two pairs of unravaged sneakers on the closet floor. Then he emptied the shredded clothes into the outside dumpster. By then, the closet was virtually empty.

Later that afternoon, he received a call from his mother. She was happy he had made it safely to Gambling. He dared not tell his mother what happened to his new clothes. They were most likely clothes she undoubtedly helped purchase. She would be furious. Louis spared her the details of the road trip. He kept quiet using only adjectives, such as adventurous and exciting, to describe the trip.

At approximately 9:00 a.m. Tuesday morning, Louis was wide awake unpacking when someone knocked on the door. "Who is it?" Louis asked.

"It is Roy the R.A. Your roommate is here. Open up."

Roommate? What, roommate? Louis thought to himself. That's when he noticed and understood why the room had two twin beds. Still, Louis did not think he would be sharing his room with another person. When he opened the door, there was Roy the R.A. standing next to Louis' roommate. A slender, athletic boy, who was just a few inches taller than Louis, stood between two suitcases. On his shoulder was an army camouflage duffle bag. In his right hand, he carried a baseball bat. On his left hand, he wore a baseball glove.

Roy said, "Louis, this is Day-Day. Day-Day this is Louis. Day-Day will be your roommate here at Attucks Hall."

The boys greeted each other with a pleasant handshake and a smile. Day-Day had an unfamiliar speech. It was different from the southern accent Louis had become familiar with from talking to Roy. Day-Day was from Greenville, Mississippi. He was on a baseball scholarship. Day-Day's energy was high. He was talkative, mostly about baseball, and how one day, he would be the star shortstop with the New York Yankees. Roy and Louis helped Day-Day drag his luggage into the room.

"If you have any questions, my room is just down the hall." Roy said. Then he calmly shut the door behind himself and disappeared.

Before unpacking, Day-Day and Louis sat on the floor and talked for hours. Other than sports, they shared experiences leading up to how they selected Grambling as their college of choice. Day-Day shared his experience first. "Grambling had a subpar baseball team with losing seasons three years in a row. They were in the rebuilding stage with a new coach. The new head coach, Coach Douglass, who is from Mississippi, had seen me play in a tournament, as a junior, in Mississippi and was impressed. He was scouting for new talent. My coach happened to be from Louisiana, and also played baseball for Grambling. He did his research, and found Grambling was in a rebuilding stage and desperately needed players. My coach made a few phone calls, sent a highlight tape, and the rest was history."

Day-Day was confident. His camouflage duffle bag was filled with plaques and trophies he had earned playing baseball. His many accolades included 1st Team All-League and Player of the Year in Mississippi.

When the two headed for breakfast the following morning, Louis learned even more about his roommate. Day-Day not only enjoyed talking about himself, but he also had swag for a boy from Mississippi. Day-Day dressed well and was a confident talker.

Day-Day was a smooth dresser. Coming out of Mississippi, he knew how to match and coordinate clothes, changing outfits, sometimes twice a day, giving the appearance he had a lot of clothes. Even the upperclassmen took notice of his many coordinated outfits.

Louis took notice of how Day-Day charmed the ladies. They would grin and giggle whenever he engaged them in conversation in the cafeteria and around campus. Day-Day was charismatic. He kept the ladies smiling with his sheepish grin and quick-wittedness. He was known for complimenting the ladies even when they didn't deserve it and even when they didn't believe it. Day-Day brought the Mississippi swagger to Louisiana. It did not hurt that Day-Day came from a household where money was rarely a problem for him. Day-Day was blessed early to have his car. As a freshman, that is special.

Louis came from a hard-working family of modest means but strong work ethics. His parents were not advocates of credit cards. Pops would preach, "If you cannot afford to pay cash, you cannot afford it."

Louis' first piece of mail came, not from his mother nor friends back home, but credit card solicitors advertising quick and easy cash to money needing college students. Louis' eyes widened. The timing was perfect. He needed money. He needed clothes. After all, it would be awkward and embarrassing for a freshman, especially coming from California, to be wearing tattered outdated gear. When people in the South think of California, they automatically think of money, fashion, and fancy cars. They would never accept Louis was from California wearing his outdated old clothes.

In no time, credit card advertisements started to arrive en masse. Credit cards followed and shopping begin. Louis started shopping in the nearby cities of Ruston and Monroe. Sometimes Louis traveled as far away as Baton Rouge when he was able to hitch a ride with an upperclassman. When Day-Day was available, Louis would invite him on these shopping sprees. Day-Day with his smooth conversation and swagger always managed to attract the prettiest sales ladies in the mail. He would make them anxious to volunteer their assistance.

Louis wanted to dress more like Day-Day, who had all the ladies' attention. Coming from California, Louis wanted to dress to impress especially with so many beautiful ladies on campus.

Louis had no idea the size of the hole he was digging for himself. He had no concept of money or financial responsibility. He was spending money he didn't have. He called home almost daily to talk to Mom and Stan. Since Louis wasn't paying the phone bill, he took the liberty to call home each day. He even called neighbors he barely spoke to even when he was in California.

Once Louis received his first credit card in the mail, his focus changed. He became a spendthrift, spending money frivolously. He spent an enormous amount of time shopping, using his charge card. Instead of being punctual to class, Louis would show up late to class so his classmates could see him stroll in with his new gear. He rarely went to the study hall. Instead spent most afternoons watching Day-Day, charming the ladies in the quad area after his amazing display of athleticism during baseball practice.

Louis wanted to be like his roommate, always surrounded by the prettiest ladies on campus. Day-Day had a large fan club, all claiming to be his study partners. Sometimes more than two of his fan club members would be waiting in the Attucks lobby after dinner, requesting to see him. Surprisingly, the girls were always gracious and respectful towards one another. They just wanted to spend time with the most popular and most handsome freshman on campus. Rarely would you find Day-Day in the Library, where the study hall was held.

Louis, on the other hand, could be found stretched out across his bed, browsing through fashion magazines, and making shopping lists of gear he was going to purchase.

Louis could not hang out on campus with Day-Day confidently until his wardrobe was up to code. Frequent visits to shopping malls in Baton Rouge, Monroe and Ruston expanded Louis' clothes closet with the latest gear. Louis' confidence grew.

***

One sunny Saturday morning after breakfast, Day-Day and Louis decided to take a ride to Baton Rouge to go to the Cortana Place Mall for clothes and to check out the females. Cortana Place Mall was bustling with people. Louis and Day-Day entered the mall near Piccadilly Restaurant, one of the most popular restaurants in the mall. After the drive from Grambling to Baton Rouge, the boys had worked up an appetite. They were hungry and decided to have lunch.

Day-Day's eyes focused on a short, brown-skin girl at the front counter at Piccadilly Restaurant. She was looking fabulous. She was Piccadilly's hostess. She was greeting customers as they entered and directing them to their seats.

"WOW!" Day-Day said. "I must get a closer look." Immediately, Day-Day went on the prowl and strolled over to make her acquaintance.

"Hello, welcome to Piccadilly's. How many in your party?" the hostess asked.

"Party of two, please," Day-Day answered looking into the eyes of the hostess with a purpose.

The hostess sensed immediately Day-Day was interested in more than just ordering food.

As Day-Day and Louis followed the hostess to their assigned seats, they watched her voluptuous hips sway from side to side. The hostess was gifted. She was perfectly shaped with a sensuous, sexy walk to match.

"Your waitress will be with you shortly, and welcome to Piccadilly. Enjoy your meal."

A short while later, another hostess walked past their table. That is when Louis' antenna went up. "Excuse me. Can we please have napkins and ketchup for our table?"

"Yes sir," the hostess replied. That is when Louis made his move.

"My name is Louis. What is your name?"

"People call me Pixie," she replied. Louis chuckled.

Day-Day asked, "What kind of name is Pixie?"

"My real name is LaTaunya. My mom nicknamed me Pixie as a child, after her best childhood friend.

"Pixie is a cute name," Louis responded, trying to get some brownie points. "This is my roommate and good friend. His name is Day-Day."

"What kind of name is Day-Day?" asked Pixie. "No mother in her right mind would name her child Day-Day."

They all laughed.

Then Day-Day said, "My real name is J'Daylin."

Pixie said, "You must be mall security or a detective J'Daylin. You sure ask a lot of questions none of which are food related."

Another waitress passed by and caught Louis' attention. "Excuse me, Miss Lady. Can I ask you your name?"

The waitress seemed annoyed. "And why do you need to know my name? You already have a waitress and have been assigned a table. Why do you need to know my name?"

"Don't mind her," Pixie interjected as the annoyed waitress passed by. "She is having a bad day. Tips aren't flowing her way. In the restaurant business, everyone is hustling, trying to make a dollar. The only attention she is probably getting is from flirtatious patrons trying to get her phone number." Pixie glanced at the annoyed waitress then winked at Louis.

The annoyed waitress turned and walked away to attend to another table. "That's how you defuse problems in the restaurant business, avoid potential conflicts," said Pixie.

Louis was impressed with how Pixie handled the situation. She was not only a cutie, but a shrewd diplomat with admirable people skills.

"Can I have your number?" Louis asked.

"How about you give me your number," Pixie responded.

Louis gladly wrote his number on a napkin and discreetly handed it to Pixie. For Louis, the game was over, time to move on. Louis was a bona fide girl watcher. Even in a smooth flowing conversation with a beautiful lady, his eyes continued to roam the food court for more cuties.

Across from Piccadilly was the Men's Apparel shop. Behind a glass counter, stood another cutie. Pixie noticed the direction of Louis' roaming eyes. "You like what you see?"

Louis was startled when he realized Pixie was monitoring his every move.

Pixie continued, "The girl in the Men's Apparel shop, you like her?"

Louis was embarrassed. "Actually, you too look alike," he replied. "Both shapely, with pretty brown skin and sexy lips." Louis tried to avoid reality, he was only at the mall to chase girls and collect phone numbers.

"If you are looking at the girl standing in the doorway at the Men's Apparel shop, just across the way, that's my younger sister," Pixie said.

"Does your younger sister have a name?" Day- Day inquired.

Pixie replied, "Her name is Peaches."

"Who names a child Peaches?" Day-Day asked.

"You can ask her yourself, when and if you two formally meet. She is nice and easy to talk to," assured Pixie. "Let me invite her over. She is looking this way."

Louis and Day-Day could see from across the food court that Peaches was also a cutie. She had a shapely body like a coke bottle with curves in the right places. Pixie introduced Louis and Day-Day to Peaches. Immediately Pixie could see the gleam in her sister's eye. Pixie could tell right away that Peaches was attracted to Day-Day. Peaches eyeballed Day-Day's muscular athletic frame from head to toe, licking her lips with an appetite.

"Why do they call you Peaches?" Day-Day asked.

She said, "They call me Peaches because I am sweet."

"I would like a bite out of that juicy peach," Day-Day mumbled under his breath glancing at Louis with a sheepish grin. Day-Day continued, "Nice to meet you. WOW! You ladies are gorgeous, like twins. How did you two ladies manage to find jobs at the same mall so near the food court?"

"Luck, I suppose," Peaches responded. "We've both worked part time at Cortana on weekends for the past two years."

"What do you two do the rest of the time, when you are not working?" Louis wanted to cut to the chase and ask questions related to dating. Louis had his eyes fastened on Pixie particularly after her diplomatic display at Piccadilly's.

Pixie, being diplomatic and changing the subject said, "We are students. We attend Southern University. We are proud Jaguars."

"And we are Tigers from Grambling, fighting tigers," Louis responded." We are here in Baton Rouge, shopping. Nice to meet you both."

Pixie and Peaches agreed to join Louis and Day-Day for lunch later that afternoon. The topic during lunch was the Bayou Classic. They decided to hook up again for the Grambling vs Southern Bayou Classic, less than six weeks away. Day-Day carried the conversation, he was the smooth talker. It was Day-Day who drove down from Grambling in the souped-up blue Dodge Charger sitting in the parking lot. It was Day-Day that had the fat savings account with deposits made weekly by his parents. It was

Day-Day that had dreams of one day playing professional baseball with the New York Yankees.

Louis wanted to redirect the conservation showing he had money. Knowing ladies like money, Louis wanted to show he had plenty. Louis spent money like water, making sure Pixie saw his new gold credit card only awarded to people with good credit. Louis wanted to wear the nicest outfits and be considered one of the best dressed wherever he went, including the mall in Baton Rouge. He purchased several outfits while in the mall and treated everyone to lunch including Day -Day. The girls took notice of Louis' kindness.

Over the next few weeks, Louis' money was slowly under pressure. He had reached his credit card limit. He was hopelessly in debt with his credit cards as a freshman. His unpaid debt quickly became a financial nightmare. It took years before he learned how an unpaid debit negatively impacted one's credit score. He remembered how it felt when he invited a cutie out on a date and handed the waitress his credit card for payment, only to discover the card was declined. Eventually, he learned money management, how not to carry gobs of credit card debt. He wanted people to believe he was coming from money. But he learned, from his roommate Day-Day, perception is all there is. Thankfully Louis didn't have any credit card woes when he was with Pixie from the mall.

One weekend, Louis and Day-Day had fun with Pixie and Peaches. Louis hadn't felt that way with another female since Marcie, back in high school. Pixie was naturally beautiful and sweet, no mascara, no makeup. Her smile was radiant and confident. She had legs like Olympic gold medalist, Wilma Rudolph, shapely and athletic. Pixie was eye candy. She wore only pink lip gloss that accented her luscious lips. It was easy for Louis to imagine caressing her in a sensuous embrace creating fireworks.

The evening was late. Louis almost forgot he had a quiz scheduled first thing Monday morning in a class where his grades were poor. He couldn't afford to be placed on academic probation. Scoring poorly on this quiz meant academic probation was a real possibility. So, the boys needed to hurry back to Grambling.

Louis hugged Pixie respectfully and gave her a soft peck on the lips. Day-Day kissed Peaches on the lips, hoping to savor sweet juices. Day-Day and Peaches held each other tightly as though they had envisioned getting a room and spending the night; then leaving early the next morning.

The ride back to Grambling was thought provoking. They laughed and joked the entire trip back to campus. Already they were missing their new friends and anxious to reconnect at the Bayou Classic, the game of the year, Grambling vs Southern.

The trip was fast with few vehicles on the dark highway. They arrived on campus just before midnight. The campus was pitch dark. They wasted no time hopping in bed. They had an eventful day. There was much to chatter about as they folded their arms behind their heads, and flopped in bed, staring up into the dark ceiling. Minutes later, the room was quiet. Louis and Day-Day had dozed off to sleep.

Sunday morning was busy. The boys were starving. They needed food. The first stop was the student cafeteria for breakfast. The hot grits, eggs, bacon, biscuits, chocolate milk, and juice were satisfying. It all had to be gobbled down quickly because church service started in 15 minutes.

In church they were fatigued from ripping and running the night before. They dozed off in church but heard the message loud and clear. They paid their tithes, sang along with the youth choir, yawning between verses. But they managed to stay awake during service.

After service, the boys lined up, turned towards the center aisle, and patiently waited their turn to walk toward the rear of the church. They shook hands with the Pastor and First Lady, then grabbed their coats from the coat rack. They quickly dashed out of the church and headed to the car. They needed to get lunch before study hall.

Fried chicken, grilled cheese sandwiches, tuna sandwiches, French fries and fresh fruit was the typical menu for lunch at Grambling. Louis and Day-Day ate hardily, and they didn't have to rush. They chewed their food slowly and properly. They were back in full strength, fully recovered from a night of excitement in Baton Rouge. They were ready for study hall.

Louis decided not to invite Day-Day to the study hall. Louis knew Day-Day would cause a distraction by chatting with the ladies. This was crunch time. Louis needed to muster all his energy to focus and remain focused for at least 3 hours. Louis' English class was first thing in the morning. He needed to perform well on the quiz.

Louis went to study hall alone carrying only his textbook and writing utensils. His mind was razor sharp, focused. He spread out his books on an empty table, hoping it would signal to all that he did not want to be bothered. Even by himself, his table filled fast with girls. Girls he had never seen on campus before. They qualified as cuties. He wished he had invited Day-Day along. He would have preoccupied the girls with his smooth conversation and sense of humor. He would have easily steered the girls to another table so that Louis could resume studying in private, uninterrupted.

"Would you mind if I used this entire table for myself? As you can see my stuff is spread out everywhere," Louis made the request as respectfully as possible. The ladies obliged, all except one who made space at the corner of the table, anyway.

"It will only be for a minute. I have an exam in the morning. I need to look over my notes. I won't be long," said the girl. She was persistent. Louis liked that.

He shrugged his shoulders and replied, "Okay."

"You have an exam tomorrow morning?" she asked, as she dropped her backpack in the one empty chair separating herself from Louis.

Just as he thought, this girl wanted to chat. Quickly she becomes a nuisance, asking trivial questions, breaking his concentration. Just when he was about to excuse himself and find another table, she mentioned Professor Johnson.

Was this a coincidence? Was she referring to the same Professor Johnson?

"Excuse me. Are you by chance referring to Professor Johnson, the Freshmen English teacher?" Louis asked.

"Yes," replied the girl. "I have an exam in her class first thing tomorrow morning. I only need to review my vocabulary words. She told us last week, the test was multiple choice, and if you knew the vocabulary words she covered in class the last three weeks, you would do well."

Louis did not recognize the girl probably because he was too busy looking good, wearing his new gear, and styling in his fresh outfits.

"Are you leaving? Please don't leave. I will be quiet. I promise," she pleaded.

Now it was Louis who wanted to chitchat. "You mind if we study together?" he asked. "My name is Louis. I am a freshman from California. I'm studying for Professor Johnson's test too."

"My name is Penny. I too am a freshman. I am from Baton Rouge," she said.

"Penny? What kind of name is Penny?" he asked.

Penny replied, "My grandma nicknamed me Penny as a small girl."

"But why Penny?" asked Louis.

"My real name is LaWauna," she said. "I am the youngest child. Because Penny is the smallest denomination, I was nicknamed Penny." She continued, "I was nicknamed Penny, also, because every time my grandma would see me, I would ask her for a penny. Everyone thought it was a cute nickname. Even my mom soon started calling me Penny. After a while, the name stuck. Here I am, 18 years later, freshmen at Grambling, responding to the name 'Penny' given to me by my grandma."

They pulled chairs close together and commenced studying. Using scissors, Penny had self-made color-coded flash cards. Her pleasant smile and soft voice made it easy to focus. In less than two hours, Louis felt confident that he would score well on the English exam. He needed that confidence. It was Penny who gave him confidence.

"I am through studying," Penny sighed. "It is time for me to head back to the dormitory." Penny grabbed her backpack preparing to leave. She said, "Nice meeting you Louis. Good luck on the exam tomorrow."

"Would you mind if I walked you to your dorm? It is late and dark?" Louis offered.

Penny smiled and said, "That would be nice,"

Once they arrived at Wheatley Hall, the all-women's freshman dormitory, the first person he saw was Day-Day. His arms were draped around the shoulder of a cutie. Louis smiled, inwardly and dared not disturb his roommate. Curfew was soon to begin, and girls were required to be inside the dorm. Boys were required to leave the area. Louis and Day-Day ended up leaving the female dorm area together.

The following morning, Louis was up bright and early full of confidence and ready for class. He quickly gobbled down breakfast and went to class. He calmly settled into his seat near the front of the class. He turned to look for Penny. She was in the rear of the class smiling graciously giving him a thumbs-up.

The exam was surprisingly easy, thanks to Penny who drilled him with the flashcards the night before in study hall. He had never studied that long or that hard. The effort paid off. Louis passed the exam with a B+. He was thrilled. He searched the campus for Penny to share the good news. He found her. She too had passed, with a perfect score!

"Would you mind if we become study partners from now on?" He asked.

Penny agreed.

Grambling College was a fun school. The students' activities calendar was loaded with exciting events. To kick off the year of entertainment, funk band Earth, Wind and Fire was the headliner. They would be performing their new hit single release, "Reasons."

The concert was scheduled to be held in the old gymnasium. The gymnasium was adjacent to Attucks Hall. Rehearsal could be heard in the lobby at Attucks. At lunch earlier that day, Louis asked his study partner Penny, if she would be his date to the concert.

Louis suggested, "We can meet at the fountain in the quad, across from the gymnasium where the concert will be held."

Penny agreed. Hours before the concert, their R.A. Roy invited Louis and Day-Day to an off-campus party at a frat house. The party was invitation ONLY, upperclassmen only. Since Louis and Day-Day were so popular on campus, they received a special invitation.

"You freshmen need to learn how to party," insisted Roy. The house party was only a few miles away from campus. The atmosphere was festive. Cuties were everywhere. A strobe light flickered from the ceiling above. The music was deafening. Sweaty bodies were bumping and grinding, swaying to the rhythm of the beat. Alcohol was flowing freely. Gin, rum and coke, orange juice and vodka were the choices. Fraternity members greeted each guest with an empty plastic cup when they entered the house.

Day-Day was an occasional drinker who learned the lesson of drinking responsibly as a young boy in Greenville. Day-Day had been to several house parties with an open bar back home in Mississippi.

In California, Louis grew up learning by watching the lessons of others who had unlearned the importance of drinking responsibility. Louis had never tasted alcohol before. He had never been to a party where alcohol was served. None of his high school buddies drank. Alcohol was prohibited on campus, and it was not allowed in his parents' house. Alcohol was served at ditch parties off campus during school hours. Louis never attended.

Now, here he was at an off-campus party. Louis was not in California. He was a college student at Grambling miles away from home. Away from rules and regulations enforced by his parents, he wanted to experience something new and different.

Louis decided at his first college off-campus frat party to be free and have a sip. No sooner did he enter the house, that he was handed a plastic cup of vodka and orange juice, his first alcoholic beverage. Louis loved orange juice. Vodka was an acquired taste. After several cups of vodka and orange juice, dancing, laughing, and joking with the ladies, the room started spinning. He stumbled backwards and landed on the sofa. His head was spinning.

"Let's go. The concert will be starting soon," a loud voice came from outside. The screen door swung open and closed as people dashed out of the house scrambling for an available car seat. People squeezed tightly together, ready to go to the concert. Louis was intoxicated.

"Let's go freshmen," Louis looked around and realized he was the only person remaining in the house. Music was still blaring, strobe light still twirling. Louis sat alone on the sofa feeling sick to his stomach, bewildered, confused and drunk out of his mind. He was feeling nauseous, but well enough to meet his study partner at the fountain in the quad.

Once he reached the quad, he staggered his way to the fountain, bumping into people along the way. His head was spinning from the alcohol. Just before he reached the fountain, he stumbled and fell on the walkway face first. He rolled over onto his back and with his arms outstretched, Louis vomited all over his new sporty sweater purchased weeks earlier from the mall in Baton Rouge. People stepped around and over him laughing on their way to the concert. One person did not laugh, it was his study partner, Penny. Penny recognized Louis almost immediately when she saw him on the walkway with vomit all over his clothes. She was visibly surprised and disgusted. Her study partner, who had performed so well on his English exam days earlier, was drunk.

"Let's go girl," insisted Monica, Penny's roommate, "Your date is drunk, in no condition to escort you to the concert. Let's go, we will be late."

Louis reached desperately for Penny, urging her to wait, but his arm was too weak. It flopped uncontrollably on the walkway as Penny walked away comforted by her friends. Louis was sloppy drunk.

"Lord," he prayed as he looked up into the heavens sprinkled with stars, "If you allow me to get over this, I promise I will never drink ever again."

Louis gradually regained his composure, stood up under his own power and walked slowly to Attucks Hall which was only a few yards away. Louis took a long cold shower, had a cup- of- chicken noodle soup, and changed into a new clean outfit. He strolled to the concert, as though nothing had happened; hoping to see Penny and Day-Day inside. Earth, Wind and Fire had just finished singing their new hit single, "Reasons." The performance was electrifying. The audience cheered, as the group disappeared into a make-shift pyramid on stage.

Louis continued to wander through the gymnasium, bumping into people along the way desperately searching for his Penny. She was nowhere to be found.

The next morning, Louis woke up to a throbbing headache. Leaning over the edge of the bed nauseously. He was sick, but more ashamed that he had destroyed the image he had worked so hard to build on campus.

His roommate, Day-Day, spent the night out. He could handle his liquor, and the two cuties from the frat party he escorted to the concert as well. Day-Day's campus image had been boosted. He was the life of the party with the ladies. Day-Day knew instinctively Louis had a lousy night. Day-Day learned that Louis had fallen like a sloppy drunk before the concert. Before returning to the dorm, Day-Day stopped by Spivey's Chicken Restaurant and bought a bucket of fried chicken and fries, coleslaw and freshly squeezed orange juice for his roommate.

"Thank You, Day-Day," Louis was grateful. Louis stayed inside the entire day, recuperating. He was too embarrassed to go outside. He was unable to reach Penny by phone to apologize.

Louis kept his promise. He never drank alcohol ever again.

Chapter 12

Bayou Classic

Louis learned a lot in his first semester in college. The importance of punctuality he learned from his Freshman English Teacher. She scolded him publicly and taught him the importance of always being on time. He learned about relationships and how blessed he was to have a friend, like Day-Day as a roommate. From Pixie, who he admired a lot, he learned how to be diplomatic and straightforward.

But he never buried the past relationship with Marcie. He thought about Penny his study partner, who had a warm, caring spirit, and was always willing to help. For a moment he entertained the thought that maybe he and Penny could evolve into a serious relationship and become boyfriend and girlfriend. Her gentle smile was good medicine for his broken heart. The thought quickly vanished when he recalled the hurt, he suffered while with his high school first love, Marcie. Louis wondered if Penny suffered a similar embarrassment when she saw him sprawled out sloppy drunk in the quad, on their very first scheduled date. Louis tried several times early Sunday evening to reach Penny by phone. Still there was no answer. He decided to walk to her dormitory Sunday after church, hoping to catch her lounging in the lobby with friends.

He waited in the lobby nearly two hours, but she was a no-show. He stayed until curfew. No Penny. Disappointed, he walked back to Attucks Hall in the dark alone hoping to cross her path along the way. He decided to wait until Monday to catch up with her in the cafeteria. If not, surely, he would see her in class. He saw her roommate, but Penny was absent. She never missed class. Her roommate refused to talk after class.

Louis began to worry. That evening, after dinner, he went to study hall. If he could decipher the 100 vocabulary words, discussed throughout the semester, on a multiple-choice examination, he would surely pass Freshman English. Louis prepared colorful flash cards like what Penny used.

Weekly Day-Day and Louis had study hall either in the lobby of Attucks Hall or in their dorm room. Louis learned several words rather quickly studying with his roommate i.e., reverence, debt, and balance sheet. He was focused, memorizing vocabulary words easily. Even though Louis was comfortable with Day-Day as a study partner, he missed his Penny. He missed her enthusiasm, her energy, and her smile. She was more than just a study partner; Penny was his closest female friend on campus. He trusted her. Every evening Louis would visit Wheatley Hall hoping to see his Penny.

Day-Day listened intently to Louis share his past female problems in their dorm room. Day-Day wanted to console his friend. To do that he decided to share a personal experience of his own. Day-Day began, “I, too, had a similar situation with a cutie back in Greenville. She was upset I was going off to college. She cried. She would call my mother almost daily crying on the phone. As I was packing to leave for Grambling, she drove up unexpectedly.

"What is she doing here, " I said to myself. She stepped out of the car, music blaring and handed me a gift bag and a card. The card read:

Wherever you are Day-Day, you will always be my love.

She then kissed me on the cheek, turned, got back into her car and drove away. Inside the gift bag was a bracelet with my name Day-Day."

"You must have been touched," Louis said.

Day-Day agreed, "I was touched. I did not realize her feelings for me were so strong. After all, we were not in an exclusive relationship. Sure, we hung out a few times, went to a few house parties together but never did we discuss being exclusive."

Louis was puzzled, "What does exclusive mean?" he asked.

"Exclusive means you and the other person have mutual feelings and have discussed and agreed to be in a one-on-one relationship," answered Day-Day.

Then it clicked. Louis and Marcie had never discussed exclusivity, being boyfriend and girlfriend. The two simply hung out together on campus and talked occasionally on the phone. They had never even gone on a date, not even to the movies or for ice cream. Louis and Marcie never talked about a relationship, he reflected. It was an awakening.

"You mean, you and your lady back home never agreed to a one-on-one relationship?" Louis asked for clarity.

"Nope," Day-Day responded without hesitation. "I told her several times, I just wanted to be friends."

Louis sat up in his bed, looking at Day-Day for his truth.

Day-Day continued, "I had other lady-friends in Greenville who I hung out with occasionally. Some I would sometimes walk to class, but nothing serious." Day-Day said, "I never let any of them believe we were anything other than just friends."

Louis was stunned. Day-Day's experience was strikingly similar to Louis' relationship with Marcie. All these years of being angry, thinking he had been betrayed, embarrassed by his first love who in all actuality was at best, a friend. In his heart, Louis had wanted to believe that he and Marcie were a couple.

Louis was still learning about relationships, peer pressure, not to be a follower, and creating his personal style and fashion. More importantly, he learned the importance of developing good communication skills. Don't be afraid to ask for what you want, and don't assume the other person is a mind reader. Time spent with Penny taught Louis a valuable lesson about relationships. He liked Penny as a friend and a study partner but not as a girlfriend. Louis realized after listening to Day-Day, Penny probably had other ideas in mind. But that too was an assumption.

Penny forgave Louis for being sloppy drunk, embarrassing her in front of her dormmates.

Penny told Louis, "Perhaps it would be better if we remain cordial. Say hi and bye in class or on campus."

Louis asked, "Can we still be study partners?"

Penny replied, "Better we cancel being study partners as well."

Louis was disappointed, but he understood Penny's reasoning and accepted her decision. From the brief time spent with Penny, Louis matured as a person and as a young man. He learned to respect other people's feelings. Louis knew he needed a mature responsible woman in his life, a relationship with substance. Not an imaginary, made up relationship, but a relationship with an understanding, with no hidden agendas. He wanted to be in an exclusive relationship.

The phone rang. Louis did not recognize the voice on the other end at first. "Hello, this is Pixie, the proud Jaguar from Baton Rouge. You and Day-Day still coming down for the Classic, for the annual Grambling beat down? You know the game is in two weeks."

How could Louis forget the cutie he met at the mall in Baton Rouge awhile back? He was surprised she remembered him.

"Of course, I remember you," Pixie said.

"The diplomat right," he chuckled. "Sorry, you chose Southern University, but I won't hold it against you." Louis replied. Louis had matured since they saw each other last. He had a clearer sense of what he wanted in a relationship. He admired straightforwardness in a girl, someone who spoke her mind with problem-solving skills. He realized to get the right answers, he needed to ask the correct questions. Louis was looking for a girlfriend, a one-on-one relationship. He wondered: What were her interests? Did Pixie just want to have fun and hang out for the weekend? What was her motivation and how did she define fun?

Louis barely knew Pixie but enjoyed the time they spent together at the mall, joking, and laughing. He remembered, Mom always said, the quickest way to a woman's heart is through laughter. If you can make her laugh, you can make her happy. Truer words were never spoken.

Louis was curious and wanted to know more about Pixie. He wanted to keep her laughing without making her uncomfortable in their undefined relationship.

Louis wondered: Was she already in a relationship? Did her boyfriend have a girlfriend? How did she feel about long-distance relationships, especially a nemesis from Grambling? All these thoughts scrambled through his brain like eggs. He had two weeks to unscramble his thoughts and sustain a lively atmosphere. What better place than at the Bayou Classic

***

The pageantry of the Bayou Classic highlighted Louisiana's HBCU Southern University Marching band, commonly referred to as the Human Jukebox, versus the world-famous Grambling College Tigers Marching band. They rocked the Superdome in New Orleans. These Southwest Athletic Conference (SWAC) powerhouse teams were fighting for bragging rights for the year.

This was the first-time Day-Day and Louis attended the Bayou Classic. The atmosphere was electric. Sounds of the Southern University Human Jukebox deafened attendees in the parking lot. Inside was even better and louder! The crowd packed the stadium and took the volume up even higher. People were on their feet screaming and hollering for their team. Vendors displayed and sold an array of Jag gear, Tiger gear, memorabilia mugs, Jaguar pom-poms and Tiger pom-poms.

Louis and Day-Day stopped at the concession stand as they entered the stadium. They purchased hot dogs, sodas, and nachos before securing their seats. They were engulfed in a friendly state of family rivalry. Overall, the stadium was an integrated sea of Southern University's Columbia blue, and gold seated alongside Grambling College's black and gold.

Even though everyone was seated together, you knew by the stadium colors which school had the largest crowd. The Superdome was dominated by Columbia blue and gold of the Southern University Jaguars. The Human Jukebox of Southern

University was surrounded by fans dressed in Columbia blue and gold in that Jaguar section.

On the other side of the field was the World-Famous Tiger Band. It was surrounded by students and alumni wearing black and gold attire, cheering for the Mighty Tigers. You could tell where the Grambling Tigers' rooting section was by its black and gold pom-poms waving in the air throughout the game. The music from the two bands and cheers from the crowd was deafening.

The crowd applauded and cheered for their favorite team during the game. However, the best part of the Bayou Class is halftime. The Superdome rocked the loudest during halftime when the bands took the field for the Battle of the Bands. During halftime, the stadium roared, screamed, and danced enthusiastically during the halftime performances. The Human Jukebox of Southern University versus the World-Famous Grambling College marching band.

The judges listened carefully to the crowds' decibels to make the right decision for the best halftime performance. No matter what decision the judges made as to the winner of the Battle of the Bands, there were always boos of disagreement from the fans, just normal reactions for a rival athletic event as spectacular and famous as the Bayou Classic. Occasionally, an unruly fan, full of alcohol, attempted to spoil the festive atmosphere, to no avail.

After the game, the party continued in the streets outside as vendors surrounded the New Orleans Superdome on Bayou Classic weekend. The aroma from the vendors filled the air. Fried chicken, ribs, and homemade barbecue sauce created a finger-licking, mouthwatering atmosphere. Potato salad, beans with mixed vegetables, sodas, and beer was also available.

It did not always matter who won the game, what mattered was you had a good time; meeting new people, being invited to hotel private parties, and collecting a phone number or two from a cutie.

Louis and Day- Day had big fun at the Bayou Classic amidst the festive crowd even though they were unable to locate Pixie and Peaches. They decided to go to Bourbon Street to hang out. The most beautiful women from all parts of the country in festive spirits were partying and having fun. Private parties at hotels sold beer, daiquiris, and hard liquor.

Louis remembered the experience he had back at Gramling when Earth, Wind and Fire came to town and swore he would never drink again. Beer was offered, even hard liquor, by some cuties, under the pretense of having fun. Nonetheless, Louis politely refused and was not tempted. He kept his promise and remained sober.

They went to a hotel bustling with fans. Through the crowd, they saw Pixie and Peaches cozied up at the bar with two guys. They were all dressed in Columbia blue and gold attire laughing and having fun. Suddenly, Louis had the same dejected feeling he experienced back at Garey High School when he first saw another guy escorting Marcie to class. He thought for a moment. Pixie is not my girlfriend. We have never talked about being in an exclusive relationship or if she was possibly already in a relationship.

His emotions ran wild with speculation. Pixie was not his girlfriend, he had to keep reminding himself, just someone he met at the Cortana Place Mall and talked to once over the phone. He did feel some kind of way when he saw Pixie with another guy. He had to remind himself, repeatedly, that Pixie was only an acquaintance, nothing formal.

Because of her personality and diplomacy skills, Pixie was the girl of his choice. However, Louis realized at that moment that Pixie was already in a committed relationship with the star Jaguar quarterback. Less than an hour earlier, this guy scored the winning touchdown that defeated Grambling. Louis nearly regurgitated in disgust when saw Pixie at the bar with her arms wrapped around her boyfriend. Louis wished it were him wrapped in Pixie's arms instead. He bowed his head and left the bar.

After the Earth, Wind and Fire concert, the Bayou Classic at the Superdome in New Orleans, and the home games, and fraternity and sorority parties, life on campus was pretty mundane.

Chapter 13

Study Hall

It was the fourth quarter and no timeouts. Time to crack the books. Finals week was coming soon. The library was packed.

Day-Day could no longer afford to spend time tutoring Louis. Day-Day was teetering on academic probation. Louis was soliciting for another study partner. What better place is there to find a study partner than in the library, in the study hall.

Sitting alone in the study hall was a slender brown skin cutie. Louis approached her study table and said, "Excuse me, do you mind if I share this table with you? I promise not to talk." Louis giggled to himself remembering when someone said almost the exact thing to him not so long ago when he needed uninterrupted study time.

"Sure," said the cutie. She pushed her books to the side that were sprawled over the table. The cutie was so engrossed in her studies, she never bothered to look up and make eye contact with Louis. Just before study hall was over, Louis introduced himself.

"My name is Louis by the way. I am a freshman from California. Thank you for allowing me to share your table," he said.

"No problem. My name is Sheila. I too am a freshman. I am from Sweetwater, Texas," she responded.

Louis asked, "Is this where you study most afternoons?"

Sheila seemed annoyed with the frivolous questions, and hurriedly packed her belongings, pushed her chair in and left the library without even saying goodbye.

That's rude, Louis thought to himself. Perhaps unknowingly he had offended her. If she is here in study hall tomorrow around the same time at this same table, he promised himself, he would comment on her rudeness at the school where the motto is: Everybody is somebody.

Back in the dormitory. Louis shared with Day-Day what he felt was rude, unacceptable behavior from a fellow female Gramblinite. After hearing the story, Day-Day yawned in boredom, covering his mouth before uttering his thoughts. "Don't sweat the small stuff," Day-Day said and that was his only advice.

Louis decided to approach Sheila the way a lion approaches a gazelle, carefully. He decided to jot down a few questions, questions he had asked girls before, and had favorable and immediate responses.

Louis recalled Day-Day saying, Girls like to talk. Ask questions that will prompt them to want to talk. While they talk, you listen. And if they don't take the bait, ask them to elaborate.

First, Louis needed clarity on why Sheila rudely left the table without at least saying goodbye. The following evening, Sheila was in study hall at the same table, alone.

"Good evening, Sheila. Hope you're having a blessed day. I was surprised you left the table yesterday without at least saying goodbye. Guys have feelings, too," said Louis. "Did I offend you?" He continued. Louis was on the offensive. "If I did, please accept my apology. Please forgive me," Sheila responded to the warranted accusation. "I didn't mean to be rude. I had a thunderous headache yesterday probably because I did not sleep well the night before and was exhausted. It is I who owe you an apology".

"Apology accepted," Louis said.

They both smiled. Louis decided to postpone his initial question until the following day believing he would see Sheila again.

When the following evening came, Louis was ready. He began, "Good evening, Sheila. Did you sleep well last night? How does your head feel today? You still have a headache?"

"I slept well last night, thank you for asking," Sheila replied, "Miraculously, the headache has gone away. Thoughtful of you to ask."

Out of the blue, Louis asked, "Are you dating anyone?"

"No," responded Sheila, "Why do you ask?"

Louis began, "Because I don't want to be talking to you and your boyfriend pops up. That could be potentially awkward."

Sheila chuckled. "Yes, that would be awkward."

They both laughed.

Louis heaved a sigh of relief. He felt like he was communicating for the first time. Sheila continued, "No worries, Louis, I do not have a boyfriend. I am here to get my degree. People back in Sweetwater are relying on me to finish school, especially my grandma. A boyfriend can be a distraction."

Louis realized the wisdom in preparing such questions beforehand. He was not yet ready, nor confident to talk to ladies without a script. The good news is Sheila was not dating and did not have a boyfriend. The bad news is it sounded like Sheila did not have time for a boyfriend and had a wise grandmother as a mentor.

The next question would be critical. Louis needed an expert opinion. No better person to discuss the situation with than his roommate Day-Day who had a variety of female friends and a lot of experience. Surely, he would offer good advice. Later, Louis told Day-Day, "I asked Sheila if she had a boyfriend or if she was in a committed relationship."

"And what did she say?" asked Day-Day. "Does she have a boyfriend?"

Louis said, "According to her family back in Sweetwater, boys are nothing more than a distraction. She promised her family, especially her grandmother, she was in college to get a degree, not a boyfriend."

Louis needed a game plan. "What is the next question?" Louis asked.

"Ask her on a date; nothing too extravagant, something simply." Day-Day advised.

Louis suddenly recalled his mother's words of wisdom, "It is the little things that matter most in life, especially with a woman."

"I think I will ask her for a lunch date," Louis decided.

"Good idea," said Day-Day. "Instead of going to the chow hall for lunch, take Sheila to Spivey's Fried Chicken. They have good food. Most importantly, Spivey's prices are affordable. For a family-size bucket of 18 chicken wings, coleslaw, and potato salad, for two, you will have plenty left over. Also, Spivey's is within walking distance of the campus."

Louis rehearsed his presentation in the mirror several times the night before he posed the question. He rehearsed on his roommate to be sure his tone and body language was proper.

The next day, Louis and Sheila had breakfast together. They ate pancakes, bacon and eggs with juice and hot chocolate.

Louis asked, "How about we do something different for lunch this afternoon?"

"Like what?" Sheila asked.

"How about we go to Spivey's Fried Chicken this afternoon for lunch. The food is delicious," assured Louis, using his most convincing tone he had rehearsed in the mirror the night before. "It will be fun and different."

It sounded corny, but Sheila agreed and that's all that mattered. Louis felt he was the champ of the world. He couldn't wait to tell Day-Day the good news. Louis wasn't sure what to wear on the lunch date with Sheila. So again, he consulted with Day-Day.

"Keep it simple," advised Day-Day. "Be sure not to overdress and be sure your outfit is in season and weather appropriate."

Louis picked Sheila up at her dormitory. She looked amazing! Her hair was freshly flat ironed. She wore a colorful dress and cute sandals, matching her manicure and pedicure. He didn't even have to wait. Sheila was in the lobby ready when he arrived looking good and smelling delicious.

It was just before rush hour. So, the timing was good. Spivey's still had several seats available for dining-in. The atmosphere was perfect. The music was mellow. Louis felt empowered for the first time taking a lady out on a formal date, albeit for lunch.

Nonetheless, he felt good and from the smile on her face, Sheila felt good too. Lunch was pleasant, no expectations, just good eating and good conversation. Louis envisioned such a moment with Marcie back in high school, but he never asked her out formally on a date.

With Sheila, it was a day to remember. They spent the entire day talking, laughing, and sharing dreams. No scripted questions were needed. After lunch. Louis walked Sheila back to her dorm. Later that evening, they both met at study hall. They were focused. There was no small talk. They studied until closing.

On Monday, Louis walked Sheila from her dorm to breakfast then to class. Louis and Sheila had found something special. Being together with no agenda. No hidden agenda made time together pressure free. From that day forward, Sheila would call Louis every night, like clockwork. They would engage in small talk, and she would bid him a good night and pleasant dreams. Sometimes the two would fall asleep on the phone.

Louis began calling Sheila every morning. "Good morning, see you at breakfast".

Sheila, in turn, would call Louis every night asking the same question, "How was your day?"

He learned to elaborate in his responses. He would then ask, "You have a lot of homework?"

The two would talk on the phone every night, joking and laughing. The conversation would not end before they prayed. Louis began feeling his time with Sheila had grown into a formal committed relationship. He was escorting her to class, the same way he used to escort Marcie to class in high school.

The following Saturday, Grambling was scheduled to play Southern in basketball at Grambling. It would be the last home game of the semester. Pixie and Peaches decided to make a surprise visit to Grambling to watch the final game of the semester and hopefully to see Day-Day and Louis to exercise bragging rights after the Jaguar victory over Grambling at the Bayou Classic. When Pixie and Peaches arrived in Tiger town, they had lunch at Spivey's.

Meanwhile, Louis and Sheila made their way to the game. The old gymnasium was packed. Day-Day entered the arena accompanied by two Gramblinite cuties. Day-Day found Louis with Sheila enjoying soda, nachos, hot dogs and popcorn. As Louis handed the popcorn to Day-Day, Louis noticed Peaches and Pixie in the center of the Jaguar cheering section on the opposite side of the gymnasium amidst the boisterous crowd. Louis nudged Day-Day and pointed in the direction of Peaches and Pixie on the other side of the gymnasium.

"We lost the Bayou Classic, but we will definitely win tonight's game" yelled Day-Day confidently across the gym.

Louis was uneasy being in the presence of Sheila and Pixie. Having feelings for both was awkward. Sheila was his lady and the person he spent most days and evenings with. They talked on the phone every morning and night, and even ate together regularly. Louis sat directly across from Pixie on the opposite side of the gym, looking almost straight in her face. Louis had never been in a situation such as this. It was indeed awkward. Louis was uncomfortable, thinking he might run into Pixie after the game with Sheila on his arm or worse yet, right in the middle of halftime.

During halftime, fans normally congregated and intermingled in the snack bar area. Peaches might see Day- Day and it would be all good. It did not matter if Day-Day saw Peaches. They were only friends. Day-Day had no romantic relationship with Peaches. They flirted with one another at the mall. Talked on the phone once or twice. They even kissed once. However, they were not boyfriend and girlfriend. In fact, Day-Day looked forward to seeing his Jaguar rival. They had not spoken in weeks. Day-Day was in his comfort zone. He felt comfortable introducing Peaches to his Gramblinite entourage. After all, it was only a basketball game, and they were only friends.

Things were different for Louis. He had what he always wanted, a one-on-one relationship. They were now together for the final game of the semester eating popcorn from the same bag, sipping soda from the same straw, cuddling together like boyfriend and girlfriend.

So now, in the middle of halftime, the concession area was flooded with fans. Amid the crowd, Peaches spotted Day-Day. With exhilaration, she ran with both arms outstretched hugging him. A casual observer could easily assume Day-Day and Peaches were boyfriend and girlfriend in a committed relationship. Day-Day embraced Peaches so tightly, she was literally gasping for air.

"Put me down. I can't breathe," Peaches pleaded, smiling.

Day-Day then turned and introduced Peaches to his friends as his fan club. "They love baseball," he declared. "They attend every home game and are my supporters. When they are in the bleachers cheering me on, I always perform well. If these ladies were at the Bayou Classic, and I were playing, we would have most definitely won. They are winners," Day-Day continued, "and that is why they are with me tonight, as an assurance that Grambling will be victorious, and that is why we are ahead at halftime," he bragged, pointing to the score board that displayed Grambling with a double-digit lead at halftime.

The ladies were gloating with pride. Day-Day was charming as always. His words were like music to the ears of his fan club and did not offend his archrival. Peaches understood her relationship with Day-Day. It was only platonic.

Louis, on the other hand, was fidgety when the moment came to introduce Sheila and Pixie. His palms perspired profusely. He was visibly nervous. Had an emotional connection with both Pixie and Sheila. Sheila noticed Louis grinning when he saw Pixie in the concessions area. Sheila excused herself, before their formal introduction. "I will be back," Sheila informed Louis, "I am going to the ladies' room." Then Sheila disappeared into the crowd.

This was a perfect opportunity for Louis to hug Pixie without restraint, share a few jokes and laughs for old time's sake, even a soft kiss on the cheek, without any suspicious stares from Sheila. When the horn sounded announcing the beginning of the third quarter, Sheila still had not returned from the ladies' room. She was nowhere to be found when the alarm sounded to end the game. Grambling won by the narrowest of margins. Day-Day was correct, his Gramblinite entourage were winners. When the game ended, it was getting dark outside. With Sheila nowhere around, Louis accompanied Pixie to her car, alongside Day-Day and Peaches.

"We are headed back to Baton Rouge tonight," Pixie announced. This was a turnaround trip to watch the game and see our Grambling buddies.

Louis warmly embraced Pixie in the parking lot in the dusk of the evening. While Day-Day was trying his hardest to convince Peaches to spend the night for old time's sake. When Pixie and Peaches finally drove off, Louis wondered whatever happened to Sheila?

Day-Day asked, "Where is your girl? I thought she liked basketball?"

In the distance, near the fountain in the quad area, Louis noticed a person seating alone. Curious, he approached the person only to discover it was Sheila, blowing her nose and wiping her eyes. She had been crying.

Louis asked, "What happened to you Sheila? You said you needed to use the ladies' room but never returned. What happened?"

By then, Sheila had broken down in tears. Her face was buried in her hands as she cried. The water splashing from the fountain, nearly disguised her tears when she finally raised her head. "I saw you were preoccupied with your friends," Sheila sniffled, "I did not want to interfere. So, I left."

Instantly, Louis felt her pain and embarrassment. Déjà vu. He recalled how he felt watching Macie walking with Marcus to class at Garey High School. It was heart-wrenching and painful.

"I apologize. That girl is only a friend. We met weeks ago when Day-Day and I went to the Bayou Classic." Louis said. He conveniently failed to mention that he and Day-Day had gone to Baton Rouge shopping and checking out the ladies and had planned to reconnect at the Bayou Classic. "They attend Southern University. They came to watch the game. No cause for alarm baby, you are my girlfriend," Louis said reassuringly.

Sheila listened intently to what Louis had to say and recalled what she witnessed at halftime. Sheila saw how Louis embraced Pixie in the parking lot. Sheila knew there were holes in Louis' story. Little did he know, Sheila watched them from beneath the bleachers after the game all the way to the parking lot.

Sheila never took her eyes off her boyfriend. Her heart was hurting when she witnessed the passionate hug, and the kiss in the parking lot. Sheila's intuition was keen, and she had great vision. Instinctively Sheila sensed Louis was not telling the whole truth about his feelings and how they knew one another. But because Sheila cared so much for Louis, she forgave him after the third apology.

The two left the quad area, holding hands in deep conversation. After walking several minutes, Sheila realized they had walked completely off campus. They were both in unfamiliar territory. "Where are we?" Sheila asked. You could hear and feel the nervousness in her voice.

"Relax baby," Louis replied in a reassuring tone.

"We have not walked long and; therefore, we cannot be far from campus. As long as you are with me, you have absolutely nothing to worry about," Louis proclaimed proudly.

Sheila took a deep sigh of relief.

"The moonlight knows where we are," Louis said with a debonair smile. He was proud of himself; all this smooth talk, he said without a script. They wandered behind an abandon gymnasium, not far from Grambling High School. It was now dark and spooky.

Sheila was nervous, despite his reassuring words, but she was excited to be alone with Louis. Only for a moment did her mind reflect on the words of wisdom from her grandmother who warned her about boys and how they can be a distraction.

Sheila felt the warmth of his body move closer. His manhood noticeably began pressing hard against her leg. With his arm wrapped around her tight waist, he gently pulled her even closer. He could feel the rhythm of her heart beating faster. He caressed her nipples over her blouse gently until they stood at attention.

The weather was a bit breezy. Still Louis wanted to be macho and took off his jacket, spread it out across the cold concrete next to the gymnasium door. He motioned Sheila to join him. She hesitated for only a moment. Then surrendered to her emotions. She was curious to see and feel the source of his strength.

Through his shorts, Sheila stroked his manhood gently. To her amazement, his manhood increased in size.

Only the owls could see clearly what Sheila saw that night when she unzipped his pants. She saw firsthand, up-close, and personal what her roommates would be giggly about late at night after spending time with their boyfriends. Her eyes widened with excitement when she finally saw her strength and wonder. It was her first experience. In fact, it was Louis' first experience penetrating such moisture and feeling such heavenly softness. Their first intimate moment together came naked beneath the midnight sky behind an abandoned gymnasium building, a special moment to cherish and repeat. Louis and Sheila rendezvoused in exclusivity every Saturday night, until he departed for winter break. It was their intimate hiding place not far from campus.

He wanted to share his adventure with Day-Day, but Day-Day was preparing for his own journey. He was busy packing to leave school.

"Where are you going?" Louis asked. "Finals aren't for a few weeks."

"I'm going home; going back to Greenville," Day-Day explained. "I have decided to transfer to Mississippi Valley next semester. I want to get closer to my family and friends."

"I thought we were friends," Louis said.

"We will always be friends," said Day-Day.

Louis knew he had lost a good friend and confidant. He never shared the details of his triumphant moment with Sheila. The two remained good friends. Day-Day remained a trusted advisor and confidant.

Chapter 14

The Nicest Guy

After completing his first semester at Grambling College in good academic standing, Louis returned to California with stories to tell and experiences to share. One of the first things he did was go to Garey High school where all his relationships first started. As a former student, he was granted permission to wait on campus until dismissal. He sat in the quad area talking to campus security about life at Grambling.

Louis went to Garey High for a reason. He wanted to thank Mrs. Gregoire, his counselor who dictated the letter of interest that ultimately led to him being admitted to Grambling. He wanted to show her his report card. He brought her a thank you card, and an authentic Grambling football jersey, to wear on Jersey Day held once a year at Garey High School. He wanted her to know how grateful he was for all her support. He also wanted to say hello to his favorite teacher, Mrs. McClain. He knew she collected mugs. So, he brought her a piece of The Mighty Tigers memorabilia, a coffee mug from Grambling. Subconsciously, deep down inside, he was really hoping to see Marcie, his childhood sweetheart. His wish came true.

The bell sounded for dismissal. The buses were boarding in the parking lot. Players, coaches along with cheerleaders boarded the bus. Students gathered to wish their team good luck. The last player to board the bus was Marcus, followed by Marcie in her blue and gold cheerleader outfit, looking pretty as ever. His heart skipped a beat.

After the Bayou Classic seeing beautiful ladies from all around the country, Marcie was not the jaw-dropping girl he remembered when she first set foot on campus at Garey High School. His feelings were strong but not as strong as he remembered.

Time, distance, and new experiences had seemingly replaced the details of his memories.

Marcie found a seat on the bus. She glanced out the window into a crowd of student fans. There in the crowd, she spotted Louis. Her eyes lit up. She was thrilled to see Louis. She leaped from seat, rushing to exit the bus to greet Louis.

Marcie jumped off the bus, ran and gave Louis a huge hug. Over Marcie's shoulder, Louis could see the curious expression on the face of Marcus, staring out the bus window. Louis was pleasantly surprised when he received the warm embrace from his childhood sweetheart.

"Welcome home Louis. So, happy to see you," Marcie said. "How long are you in town?"

Louis was flattered to see that Marcie was genuinely happy to see him. For him, her smile was worth the trip.

"Are you going to the game tonight?" She asked. "We are playing your alma mater, Pomona High. It is their Homecoming. You got to be there. Please come," Marcie pleaded.

Louis thought for a moment and replied, "Sure, that should be fun."

She gave Louis another hug and kiss on the cheek all the while Marcus was watching from the bus window. "See you at the game." She waved goodbye and hurriedly boarded the bus.

From the bus window, Marcus carefully eyeballed the entire reunion between Louis and Marcie.

Louis walked back on campus with a smile. He looked forward to Homecoming.

While on campus, he wanted to say hello to his favorite teacher, Mrs. Powell. When he finally reached her classroom, she was locking up preparing to leave campus.

"Louis, my hero," she yelled and greeted him with a warm hug. "Welcome home. I heard you were back in town. Are you coming to the game tonight? Let's sit together in the bleachers. I would love to learn more about Grambling and life in the South. Perhaps you can come to talk to my class about life in college, next week. They all know you and would be delighted to hear your college experiences."

"Anything for you, Ms. Powell. I will be delighted to come talk to your class," said Louis.

The game couldn't come soon enough. Louis was anxious. He decided to wear his authentic Grambling College Jersey to the game, showing no allegiance to either Garey or Pomona High. He was no longer in high school. He was a college student, who just completed his first semester at Grambling.

It was Pomona High School's Homecoming. First, he chose to sit on the side of Garey High School. In the second half, he sat on the side of Pomona High, his Alma Mater.

Louis felt like a hero, coming home from war. Little did they know, his first semester in college was a battle.

At halftime, cheerleaders customarily cheer on the opponent's side of the field. Louis was beaming with pride when his name was announced, and he walked onto the field with all the newest Pomona alumni in attendance. Louis spotted Marcie out of the corner of his eye, on the field in her blue and gold outfit cheering for Pomona High's newest alumni. The experience was surreal. From both sides of the stands, when his name was called, there was thunderous applause.

When the alumni returned to their seats seated just behind Louis was a boisterous fan. He distinctly overheard a fan seated just behind him admiring the halftime festivities, especially the Garey cheerleaders.

WOW, look at her, second from the end!"

Louis focused his eyes on the cheerleader, second from the end. It was Marcie, swinging her athletic legs high in the air in unison with the cheer squad. Louis heard the fan describe Marcie's physical features, her shapely athletic legs and gorgeous smile. Listening to the fan, Louis couldn't help but reminisce when he first saw Marcie. When she walked into the main office, he too was mesmerized, describing her in the same way.

"I would like to get a closer look," the fan shouted.

"Someone that beautiful surely has a boyfriend," another fan commented.

When he saw Marcie in that blue and gold cheer outfit, he knew his feelings for her were still strong. His alma mater won the game, in overtime. Once the game ended, Louis watched Marcie to see if she would find her way to the end zone where the visiting team players customarily gathered before heading to the bus. But Marcie scanned the bleachers on both sides of the stadium searching.

Louis and Marcie's eyes finally made contact. He was near the concession area with a box of popcorn in hand. Marcie jogged in the direction of the concession area to greet Louis when suddenly, out of nowhere, Marcus appeared with shoulder pads and helmet in hand.

Marcus hugged and kissed Marcie passionately. What he witnessed was no assumption.

Louis froze, his face dropped. Once again, his high school sweetheart had eluded him.

"Never walk backward, '' he recalled Day-Day saying, "you may fall, and get hurt."

The following Monday, Louis went back to Garey High school, only this time, to be guest speaker in Ms. Powell English class.

There were no absentees. The entire class stood and applauded when Louis entered the classroom greeting Ms. Powell with a huge hug.

Louis motioned for the class to be seated. "Thank you, Ms. Powell, for inviting me to share my college experience with your class. Thank you again, Ms. Powell," Louis bowed in reverence. The class applauded, sharing his sentiment. "As this is an Advanced Placement English class, I find it important to share a few vocabulary words, words I found to be important in describing my college experience. The first word is reverence. What does reverence mean?" Louis asked the class.

A few students raised their hands eagerly with good answers, but not the answer Louis was seeking. A student in the rear of the class looked up the word reverence, stood, and read the definition aloud so all could hear, "Reverence means to have a deep respect for someone or something."

Louis smiled and said, "Starting with your parents, teachers and elders including your college professors. I know some of you are not fond of some of your teachers. That doesn't matter. Learn how to eat the meat and spit out the bones. You do not have to like your teachers to learn. In my case, I learned reverence from my Pops on the two-day road trip to Grambling. I also learned that money doesn't grow on trees."

His mother often used that last phrase when Louis called home asking for money. The students were familiar with the phrase and quickly understood.

Louis continued, "Credit is the second word," Louis continued. He elaborated on his experience with credit. "You are in college to learn. It is not a fashion show. You are not looking for the best dress award on campus. Fashion changes regularly. To keep up with the latest fashion requires money. I made the mistake and applied for a credit card. Free money, I thought. I charged everything, shoes, clothes, sunglasses, food etc., not realizing you must pay that money back with interest.

Borrowing money from your parents, or family member, for instance, may or may not require you to return the money by a deadline. In some cases, their loan may be forgiven.

A credit card is a loan, a loan with interest, and must be paid back."

Questions from the class were engaging.

"Stay away from credit cards," Louis warned," until you are absolutely sure you understand how it works."

From the questions posed by the class, Louis could tell they clearly had little knowledge about credit cards including its pros and cons. Louis adamantly said, "You don't spend what you don't have."

The students were on the edge of their seats, when Louis ended his discussion by talking about relationships.

Louis began, “In college, I learned many things. The most important thing is relationships. I learned frankness and communication are key ingredients in a meaningful relationship. I’m speaking to the boys. Just because you walk a girl to class, buy her lunch periodically, or you two attend a football game together, doesn’t necessarily mean she is your girlfriend.”

“Amen!” came loudly from the girls in the class, including Ms. Powell.

Louis continued, “I took the relationship test here at Garey High School and failed miserably. I took the relationship test in college. I learned from my roommate in college, to never assume anything, especially in a relationship. I learned relationships can be tricky when the parties involved have bad prior relationships. Bad relationships are like sugar poured into their engine of trust. The body looks fine, rims are polished, but a knock in the engine may signal something is wrong; something that may require an extensive diagnostic test. When you purchase a car from a used car lot, you are purchasing someone else’s problems, undetected after a fresh paint job, wheel alignment and a major tune-up. Even after a test drive, the car may sound fine, rides comfortably with leather seats and smells nice from lemon air freshener. After spending gobs of money, the car suddenly has problems.” Louis concluded, “Car lots are everywhere; new and used. Better to stay away from used car lots and focus on new cars; cars with zero miles that come with a lifetime warranty. Thank you for allowing me to share my college experiences. Does anyone have any final questions they wish to ask before I leave?”

“Yes, I have a question,” said the voice. A petite girl wearing a blue and gold cheerleader sweater sat in the back of the room with her hand raised. “You dated Marcie, who is now captain of the varsity cheerleader squad. Rumor on campus had it you two were in a relationship. Are you two still dating? And if so, how difficult is it to manage a long-distance relationship?"

The question caught Louis off guard and rattled his carefully prepared presentation. The question brought back hurtful memories. Louis was stunned at the frankness of the question.

Had the girl in the back of the class who posed the question witnessed Marcie's welcome home embrace in the parking lot before the buses left for the game? he wondered. Did she see the embarrassing expression on his face when Marcie and Marcus embraced while he stood by near the concession stand after the game? Did she notice Marcie leaving the concession area with Marcus without, at least, saying goodbye to Louis? The class listened keenly as he struggled to answer the question.

Buried in a rubble of embarrassment and shame was the question Louis hoped would not surface. He wanted his response to the question to be honest and tactful. He thought about his mother, wishing she were present to answer the question on his behalf. She knew, deep down inside, her son was embarrassed and hurt. He was looking for a place to hide so he ran off to college. Louis was tactful in his response; using his mother's word of wisdom to answer, I went to the rock to hide my face, and the rock cried out, there is no hiding place.

"Frankly," Louis admitted, "my relationship with Marcie was painful. I thought I had put the painful memory behind me. The pain resurfaced Friday night at the Homecoming game when I saw Marcie and my nemesis hugging. It was then I realized she was happy and had moved on with her life." His voice trembled. Students became teary-eyed as he told his naked truth.

"I learned a lot about relationships while in college," Louis continued. "What better place to ask good questions and get good answers than in college?"

The class chuckled.

"For what it is worth, the girl in the back of the class said, "Well, while you were at Garey, I thought you were the nicest guy on campus."

-THE END-

www.ingramcontent.com/pod-product-compliance
Lightning Source LLC
Chambersburg PA
CBHW070626310726
48982CB00001B/179

9798990858312